FOOLISH MISTAKES

JEANA E. MANN

ISHKADIDDLE PUBLISHING, LLC

 Created with Vellum

1

DAKOTA - NOW

ON A cold spring morning, I stepped into Joe's Java Junction and shook the rain from my hair. At the order counter, a tall gentleman took his cup of coffee and turned toward me. Our gazes connected with the impact of two colliding automobiles. He froze in his steps, lips pursed to blow on the hot liquid, and drew in a sharp, startled breath.

I stared into a set of familiar eyes over the rim of his cup as he took a sip. Recognition flared then extinguished in their depths. A tremor of panic shook my fingers, and I fought to maintain my composure. In all the years I'd lived in the city, I'd never once run into anyone from my past. I took comfort in the anonymity of living far from the small town where I'd grown up. In retrospect, I'd been a fool to believe my past was forgotten or that I could escape it so easily.

We stood facing each other, shocked into wordlessness, until a woman touched his arm. She was tall, slender, and immaculate in a tight black pencil skirt and high-heeled pumps. Blonde hair formed a perfect chignon at the nape of her neck. I smoothed a self-conscious hand over my brown hair, frizzy from the rain, and tried not to think about how it must look. Her gaze flicked from the man to me and back to the man again.

"Samuel?" The low, cultured tone of her voice speaking his name sent a shiver down my back. "We're going to be late."

His gaze disconnected from mine. I swallowed and stepped back, giving him a polite smile. He didn't reciprocate. Instead, he turned to the woman and nodded, his hand resting on the small of her back. The contact was warm and intimate, the same way he'd touched me long ago. My chest tightened with emotions I'd thought forgotten.

"Samuel." This time, the woman's voice held a note of annoyance.

Once upon a time, this man and I had been more than acquaintances. He'd been the center of my universe, and I'd been his wife. I knew the way his hands felt on me, the way he looked when he came during sex, the way his skin tasted in the morning after his shower. Now we were nothing more than strangers with a shared past, brushing shoulders in a coffee shop, before moving onto our respective lives.

"Miss? What can I get for you?" By the narrowing of the barista's eyes, she'd asked me more than once.

"Sugar-free vanilla non-fat latte with a double shot." Although my lips formed the words, my gaze followed the back of Sam's black trench coat out the door. He was taller than I remembered, his shoulders broader and his hair blonder. His driver met him on the sidewalk with an umbrella and ushered him to a silver BMW with blackout windows, the blonde at his side. I lifted a hand to the thin chain around my neck and fingered the plain gold band suspended on the end.

"Your change, miss?" The annoyed voice of the barista suggested she'd lost her patience with me. I tore my attention from Samuel and back to the girl frowning in front of me.

"Sorry," I said with a half-hearted smile. The girl huffed and dropped a quarter into my outstretched palm. By the time I turned back to Samuel, he was gone, but the shock of seeing him followed me out of the coffee shop and back to the office.

Every time I slid into a chair behind the mahogany conference table, my pulse beat a little bit faster. Corporate life made my blood sing like the headiest drug. I took my normal seat next to the head of the table, where Ansel, the president, would sit. It was a position of honor and one I'd worked hard to attain. From beyond the gleam of polished hardwoods and brass, my co-workers stared at me. Usually the room hummed with friendly banter. This morning an eerie silence prevailed. I was still too overcome by my encounter with Samuel to analyze the source of the quiet.

"Good morning, everyone." Ansel entered the executive conference room, his jaw clenched tight. He was a slender man; bookish glasses perched on his nose, with wisps of gray threading his brown hair. "Thank you for joining us at such short notice." The strain around Ansel's eyes caught my attention more than his words. "We'll get to the crux of the matter in just a minute." Instead of sitting next to me the way he usually did, he remained standing and shifted from foot to foot, avoiding my curious gaze. "We're waiting on one more person."

"Is everything okay?" I asked him, studying his face

with concern. "Can I get you anything?" Ansel might be demanding and overbearing, but he'd always been kind to me.

He didn't answer but patted my hand absently before turning away. I followed the trajectory of his gaze.

The smile on my lips fell away when the woman from the coffee shop strode into the room. She walked to the front and rested a hand on the arm of a man staring through the wall of windows at the blue sky outside. A man I'd failed to notice until this very second. The square set of the broad shoulders beneath an impeccable black suit brought the world to a stop for the space of an entire second. He stood with his hands shoved into his pockets, face turned away, the split of his suit jacket revealing a bite-worthy ass beneath the tailored trousers. Messy blond hair brushed the starched white collar of his shirt. When he glanced at the woman, morning sunlight glinted off random gold hairs in the scruff on his square jaw, the glare obscuring most of his face. *Samuel.* A frisson of anxiety rippled through my gut.

"I could use some coffee," Brian, head of advertising, said from my left. He leaned into my shoulder, whispering over my ear. I shivered and not in a good way. He was such a creep.

"Get it yourself," I hissed, my eyes glued to the source of my anxiety.

"But you're so good at it," he replied, unruffled by my rebuff. For reasons unknown to me, Brian continued to treat me like a receptionist, asking me to make coffee, copies, and schedule appointments for him whenever Sadie, the receptionist, was out. He wasn't a bad-looking guy, solid build, sandy brown hair, hazel eyes, and he could be charming when he wanted. He also had a reputation for sleeping with the staff, in spite of his fiancée and our company policy.

When his thigh brushed against mine beneath the table, I glared and slid my chair to the side. Sleazeball. He smirked. "Pardon me."

"Looks like we're all here," Ansel said, drawing my attention away from Brian. "We can go ahead now."

Sam turned to face the group. I lifted my coffee cup to my lips. Grass-green eyes rested on my face. Brian's thigh bumped me again beneath the table. I jerked, and the cup slipped from my fingers and landed on the table with a clank. Lukewarm coffee poured down the front of my pink silk blouse. Brian cursed and sprang to his feet, brushing at the splatters on his khaki pants. Camille, head of accounting, grabbed a handful of tissues from the credenza and thrust them at me, but I just sat there, staring numbly at Samuel.

"Dakota?" Ansel's voice drifted through the chaotic haze in my mind. A frown puckered the space between his brows. My composure snapped into place.

"Excuse me," I said. "I'll be right back."

Before anyone could speak, I sprinted out of the room and into my office. I closed the door behind me and leaned against it, pressing a hand against my chest to calm my racing pulse. It just wasn't possible, was it? How could he be here? For the second time this morning, memories better left forgotten flooded my thoughts. Sweet, drowsy kisses. Riding bicycles in the rain. Laughing over morning coffee. The painful squeeze of my chest forced me to cut them off.

"Dakota? Can I help you?" A light tap at the door and the voice of my assistant, Melody, called me to action. "Ansel said to hurry."

Of all the places in this enormous city, what was he doing here? I didn't have any idea what he'd done since our divorce or the career path he'd taken. I didn't want to know.

I'd managed to get past our morning brush at the coffee shop by shoving it deep down into the darkest recesses of my being and padlocking the door. I could hardly avoid him now. Not when he was in the next room.

I shrugged out of the blouse and pulled my jacket from the closet. With shaking fingers, I buttoned the front and took a hasty glance in the mirror on the back of the door. A bit more cleavage revealed than I preferred, but it would have to do. I opened the door, thrust the blouse at Melody, and returned to the conference room. Samuel had taken me by surprise, but I'd never let him know. I couldn't, not when I was the one responsible for our breakup.

"I apologize for the delay," I said, wearing my winningest smile. "Let's get to business, shall we?"

Ansel tapped the table, calling the room to order. "I'd like to introduce you to Samuel Seaforth, president of Infinity Enterprises. This morning, Samuel took over controlling interest of Harmony Developments and he'll be heading up the company from today forward."

The blood left my face and drained all the way into my toes. A murmur of concern rippled around the room. Samuel Seaforth was taking over the company. My company. All of my plans for the future withered and died in front of my eyes at this unwelcome revelation.

Samuel shoved his hands deeper into his trouser pockets, a gesture so familiar it brought a sharp stab of nostalgia. Our eyes met again and a tremor shook my hands.

"Thank you, Ansel," Samuel said, still staring at me. "I want to assure everyone that we mean to make this merger as painless as possible. There will be growing pains, of course, as we blend the two companies into one and reorganize the company structure. And to that end, we are asking you to reapply for your positions." He gestured to the woman at his side. "Dahlia will be conducting interviews throughout the rest of the week in order to get acquainted with each of you and determine who's best suited for the positions."

"Some of us have contracts," I interjected. Ansel had insisted I sign an employment agreement when I took the Project Acquisitions Director position. Now I had to wonder if he'd known all along about the merger and had taken steps to protect me. I cast him a grateful glance. He answered with an almost imperceptible nod.

"So you do, Ms. Atwell," Samuel said. His deep voice dwelled on the syllables of my name, and not in a good way. "You and I will discuss your situation at a later date. In private." He dismissed me with a turn of his head, addressing the rest of the room. "Now, let's talk about our future."

2

DAKOTA - THEN

THE BELL rang, signaling the end of sixth period. A dozen high school honor students, including me, shifted into motion. I jumped from my desk, feet moving toward the door as I scooped my backpack from the floor and looped my arms through the straps. I kept my head down, mind racing with thoughts of homework and responsibility while the other students smiled and laughed and cracked jokes. No one spoke to me.

The smell of polished wood permeated the venerated hallways of Seaforth Prep Academy. Locker doors banged shut. Teenaged voices buzzed, a quiet hum in the background of my mind. I paused at my locker long enough to grab my sweater then moved toward the exit along with the other students. The blond god standing by the door turned to face me. Our eyes met for the briefest of seconds when I approached. Blood rushed into my face at the attentions of the hottest guy in the school. I dropped my eyes to the floor and readjusted my backpack to ease the weight on my shoulder, discomfited by the scrutiny.

Samuel Seaforth was *that* guy. Every school had one.

The one who possessed all the positive attributes possible for an eighteen-year-old boy. The kind who looked like a man in a schoolboy's uniform. Long legs. Broad shoulders. Square jaw with the hint of afternoon shadow. The conservative cut of his navy blazer contrasted with his wavy surfer-boy hair. Khaki pants stretched over narrow hips, pulled tight by hands shoved deep into his pockets. The throat of his striped button-down gaped open, revealing a smattering of gold hair, necktie noticeably absent. I guess you could disregard dress code rules when your family's name graced the school.

Someone shoved me from behind as I reached the threshold. I pitched forward, stumbling over Samuel's pointy-toed Italian shoe. He wrapped a hand around my bicep, steadying me. The unexpected heat of his palm on my arm startled a gasp from my lips. The backpack slid from my shoulder and hit the floor with a dull thud. Stuffed to bursting, the threadbare nylon split, spilling papers and pencils into the paths of the students.

I caught a glimpse of the boy who'd pushed me and scowled at the smirk on his face. "Jerk," I muttered and bent to gather my scattered belongings. Dozens of feet trampled over my papers, leaving dirty footprints on the pristine white paper, shuffling them out the door and down the steps. With an exasperated growl, I watched the papers take flight on a spring breeze and whirl toward the street like psychotic doves. I launched out the door and tried to catch them before they were lost forever.

After a mad scramble, I stood puffing on the sidewalk, a thin gleam of perspiration on my forehead, papers clutched in my hand. I'd managed to retrieve almost all of them. My shoulders slumped a little as I dusted the footprints from the sheets and pressed them against my knee to straighten the wrinkles.

"Hey. These are yours." The deep timbre of the voice at my shoulder was unmistakable. A large hand snaked into the field of my vision, tanned fingers clasping a handful of my precious term paper. "I think that's all of them."

"Thanks." I took the papers from Samuel's hand and squinted up at him. I'd never been especially shy or quiet, but this guy was so out of my league, I couldn't do more than stammer the one word. With the afternoon sun behind him, his blond hair glowed around his head. The papers crinkled like dry autumn leaves as I shoved them into my backpack and clutched it to my chest.

"I know you, don't I?"

To my chagrin, his footsteps followed me down the sidewalk. I tucked my chin into my chest and kept walking. He might be beautiful, but he was one of them. One of the others. He was a privileged rich kid. I was nothing but a girl from the trailer park on the wrong side of town. He caught up to me in two long strides and paced at my side.

"I'm in three of your classes," I said, still not looking at him. "You sit right in front of me."

"Crockett's sister, right?"

"Dakota," I corrected.

He snapped his fingers and nodded. "Right. Dakota." He shoved his hands into his pockets and continued to walk beside me. I felt the weight of his gaze travel over me. "But I've seen you somewhere else, too, haven't I?"

"My mom is your cook," I said after a lengthy pause. "And I work in your kitchen on the weekends." I stuffed an escaping paper into the backpack and caught a glimpse of the black limousine trailing along the curb behind us. "That's yours?"

His gaze followed mine to the car. Broad shoulders lifted and dropped in a nonchalant shrug. "Yeah."

"Don't you drive a Jaguar or something?" I knew good and well he'd received a new 911 Porsche for his sixteenth birthday. I'd seen it sitting in his driveway with a bright red bow on the windshield when I'd helped my mom prepare *hors d'oeuvres* for his birthday party. Over two hundred people had attended the event and Seven Drift, my favorite band, had played. While my classmates had danced and partied, I'd scoured pans, mopped floors, and cleaned counters. When my mom had been preoccupied with the cake, I'd managed to sneak into the backyard and had hidden behind the pool house to watch the celebration unfold.

"Yeah. Well..." His gaze drifted back to my face. "I got in some trouble and my dad took it away."

"Gee, that sucks," I replied with sincere sympathy. As a voyeur to his seemingly perfect life, I never expected to find a guy with flaws. He lifted a notch in my esteem. Beautiful but imperfect. My kind of guy.

He shrugged again. "I don't really care one way or the other. It's just a car." The way he said it struck a chord in me. I understood apathy. Sometimes it was easier not to care about inconsequential things. My father's death the previous year had put life into perspective. We'd sold our home, moved into a rental, and I'd been forced to adapt to a simpler way of life.

"Right." I snorted. "To you, it's just a car. To me, it's a car that cost more than my mom's salary." And part of said salary came from Samuel's parents.

"Money doesn't mean shit, Dakota," he said. The sudden outburst brought me to a halt. We were alone by this time, except for the trailing limo. The other students had disappeared into their respective cars and limousines, leaving us alone on the sidewalk next to the bus stop.

"Only people who have money say things like that," I said, angry but unsure why. "You have no idea what it's like to be broke."

One of his sleek golden eyebrows arched. After an uncomfortable beat, he nodded. "True. But you have no idea the problems money can cause."

We studied each other, at an impasse. I squelched the urge to smooth the skirt of my uniform and stood straighter. I was tall, but he was taller. I lifted my chin and met his gaze. His eyes reflected the bright green of the grass beside us.

"I don't feel sorry for you." I'd been inside the splendor of his sprawling family home, seen the marble floors, and polished silver trinkets worthy of a museum display. To my surprise, a slow smile widened his mouth. The expression transformed his face from aloof to warm and playful.

"Yeah?" He took the backpack from me before I could stop him and strode toward his limousine. "Come on. I'll give you a ride home."

The last place I wanted to take him was my home, a dilapidated house trailer with a leaky roof and broken shutters. The entire house could fit inside his dining room. In fact, his mother's horses lived in better quarters than I did. Even though my insides cringed at the idea, I followed him to the car, mesmerized by the easy grace and confidence of his stride. He opened the door and waited while I slid inside before following me. I gave the driver an address, not my own but the convenience store around the corner where I worked part-time, and watched Samuel settle into the seat. In the confines of the car, I could smell his cologne, a mixture of spice and soap. Goosebumps prickled along my arms when one of his knees bumped against mine.

"So what did you do?" I asked to break the silence. "To lose your car, I mean?"

His hands rested on the tops of his thighs, fingers splayed. They clenched at my questions then relaxed with visible effort. "I missed one of my mother's dinner parties."

"For real? That's it?" I'd been grounded more times than I cared to count. Most recently for smoking. Twice last month for staying out too late on a school night.

The smooth skin above his brows furrowed. "It was a really important dinner party."

"What were you doing?"

A slow grin curved his mouth. I was beginning to enjoy his smiles almost as much as I enjoyed the vivid emerald hue of his eyes. Earning his approval warmed me from the inside out. He leaned forward as if about to reveal a devastating secret. "I can't tell you, but I can show you."

3

DAKOTA - NOW

B Y THE time I got to Ansel's office after the meeting, I thought I might pass out from nervous anxiety. Samuel sat in the leather chair behind the mahogany desk with his back to the door. The sight of his ruffled hair sent a shard of panic straight into my gut. My entire future rested in the hands of a man who hated me. Feeling like a prisoner about to face his executioner, I slid into the chair across from him and tried to school my features into nonchalance.

"You wanted to see me?" I asked.

He swiveled around to face me and raised a finger, indicating silence. For the first time, I saw the Bluetooth in his ear. His eyes met mine without a hint of emotion and flicked away like we were strangers. Which we were. Sort of. I smoothed the fabric of my skirt over my thighs with sweaty palms and tried to steady my fluttering insides.

With his attention focused elsewhere, I cast a surreptitious glance at him. It had been ten years since we'd been this close, and the subtle changes in his face fascinated me. There were fine lines around his eyes, and a tiny scar marred his upper lip. Dark gold scruff stubbled his cheeks where his skin had once been smooth. He'd always been attractive, but age and experience had matured him into a handsome man. More than handsome. The guy was still freaking hot. Hotter, if it was even possible. A ripple of lust shimmered through my torso and tightened my nipples. Damn nipples. I crossed my arms over my chest to hide them. He'd always had that effect on me. I guessed some things never changed.

"I don't care whose fault it is. I want you to take care of it." Samuel's words were calm, but the edge to his voice made my skin prickle with renewed alarm. This was a man used to giving orders and having them followed without question. Gone was the unassuming boy from my youth. I felt a sharp pang of longing for him—that sweet, playful boy. What had caused this dramatic shift? Something significant must have happened to catapult this change. "When you call me back the next time, the only words I want to hear from your mouth are 'it's done.'"

Samuel disconnected the call and turned the full force of his gaze onto me. We stared at each other for an interminable minute. I saw the eyes of a stranger in the face of my ex-husband. Impersonal. Assessing. Cold. He cleared his throat, and I jumped like he'd stuck me with a pin.

"Dakota." He said my name, eyes clouding, as if it were a curse word. "It's been awhile."

"Yes. It has. How've you been?" Casual words, considering the circumstances of our breakup. I heard my voice in the distance, calm and controlled, reflecting none of the turmoil churning inside me.

"Let's cut the bullshit, shall we?" His complete disregard for pleasantries caught me off-guard. I gulped. He tapped his fingernails on the desk. "We're here to discuss your future employment with Infinity Enterprises. I have a dozen acquisition managers. I need to know why I should keep you on here."

Jesus. Was this my interview? For some reason, I'd expected a Human Resources representative or a department head, not the CEO of the company, a.k.a. my ex-husband. I curled my hands into fists, determined to calm my quaking insides. I thought I'd at least have time to prepare. A second glance at his impassive face steeled my nerves. I could do this. Working under pressure was one of my best skills. I drew on it now.

"I wasn't aware this was an interview or I would have brought my resume," I said, drawing myself up straighter on the edge of my chair.

"I've seen your resume," he interrupted. "I want to know why I should forget everything I know about you and make you a part of my team. What makes you worth my time and money?" The way he said the word *money* sent heat rushing into my cheeks.

"I have a contract," I said, keeping my voice level and calm, trying not to sound smug. Internally, I thanked Ansel again for insisting on the formality of an employment agreement.

"So you do. With a non-compete clause that prevents you from working within a fifty-mile radius should your employment here end. The way I see it, if you don't take my offer, you'll be unemployed for the next two years." His lips twitched, holding back a smile. "The contract means nothing to me. If I wanted to, I could end your career with a few phone calls."

He did *not* just go there. His callous manner sparked my indignation. Dirty bastard. If that was the way he wanted to play, I was all in. "You wouldn't do that."

This time he didn't curb his grin. "I can and I would." He tapped a manicured fingernail on the desktop. "Now, convince me, and make it good."

Who was this jerk? Certainly not the laidback guy I'd married. I coughed and wished desperately for a glass of water while I tried to gather my defense.

"Today, Dakota." His finger tapped again on the desk.

"I'm sure Ansel will tell you I've been an exemplary employee. Over the past two years, I headed numerous projects and scouted eight building sites. All of them successful. I brought on three new clients, a total of five million dollars revenue in the last fiscal year, and I have several prospects for the upcoming year. I'd be happy to provide you with a copy of my projections." I paused to form my next words.

"I know all of these things already, Dakota." He stood and leaned forward over the desk, jaw clenched, and stared me down with the animosity of a lion eyeing his lunch. "What I want to know is if you've changed. How do I know you aren't going to abandon the company when things get tough? How do I know you won't sell out confidential information to the highest bidder?" *The way you sold me out.* He didn't say those last words, but I heard them loud and clear. Our noses were now inches apart, and I felt the heat of his breath on my face. A strange tingle erupted between my legs. Powerful men turned me on. I didn't want this one to know the way he affected me. I squelched the attraction by squeezing my thighs together. "How do I know you won't fuck me over again, Dakota? What kind of assurance can you give me?"

Apparently, time didn't heal all wounds. I'd hurt him, and the gash of my actions still gaped open years later. I saw it in the flash of his eyes, the muscle ticking in his cheek, and the thinning of his lips. He hated me. And I deserved it.

"You, of all people, should know there are no assurances in life," I said, a strange sense of calm washing over me in spite of my shame. He had every right to be pissed. I'd treated him horribly, left him without explanation, and been paid handsomely for doing so. For years, I'd locked away the shame of accepting a bribe, the pain of abandoning the love of my life, refusing to acknowledge it. Face to face with the victim of my actions, the ache returned, fresh and impossible to ignore. I tried to swallow down the lump in my throat, but it hung there.

He came around the desk in two long strides and gripped me by the arms, lifting me to my feet. The power in his grasp radiated through my biceps. I was tall at five-nine, but he was taller and much stronger. I tipped my head back to meet his eyes. They flashed with such fire and animosity that my heart skipped a beat.

"Uh, I'm guessing you're still pissed," I said, trying to make light of the situation and, by the tightness of his hold, failed miserably.

"When I saw your name on the employee roster, I nearly choked on my breakfast," he said. "I almost passed over this company because of it. That's how much I hate you, Dakota. But then I asked myself, what would Dakota do? She wouldn't be swayed by emotion. She'd think about the money and not the people involved."

The accuracy of his words cut me in a way I hadn't known possible. I wanted to look away, but the passion in his gaze held me. He wasn't saying or doing anything I didn't deserve. The length of his body pressed against mine. A spark of attraction arced between us. That damn undeniable spark. He might hate me, but the hardness against my belly said the physical lust remained.

"It was a long time ago, Samuel," I whispered, unable to find my full voice. "Things have changed."

"For you, maybe. But not for me." His gaze dipped to my lips and back to my eyes. "I still remember everything about that day. The way you looked, what you wore, how you smelled." He leaned forward and scented me in a way that liquefied my bones. "The way you promised to be there when I got home. The way you made love to me the night before like you meant it."

He let go of me abruptly as if the touch of my skin scalded his hands. I landed in my chair with a startled *oof*. Tears prickled behind my eyelids. I remembered everything about that day too. The way he'd smiled at me when he left for work. How I'd stood in the window and watched him leave, knowing it was forever. If only he knew how much I hated myself for what I'd done to him, how I'd cried myself to sleep for a solid six months after leaving him. How I would never forgive myself for hurting him that way.

"I did mean it. I meant all of it. I never..." I said, but he waved my words away with a sweep of his hand through the air, dismissing me.

"I'm not interested in your apologies or your excuses." The arctic cold of his tone sent a shiver down my back. "Not now." He took a seat on the edge of the desk and clasped his hands in his lap, knuckles white with the strain. "It's too late for that."

"If not an apology, then what do you want from me, Samuel? It sounds like you've already made up your mind." I stood and gathered the shreds of my dignity around me, prepared to collect my things from my office and leave.

"I have made up my mind," he said. One corner of his

mouth twitched in a sadistic smile. My stomach flipped with anxiety. "The job is yours, if you want it." Dread flooded through me. "Same pay. Same benefits. With a six-month probationary period. I'll need your decision in the morning." He returned to his seat behind the desk, his focus turning to the laptop at his elbow. "That's all, Ms. Atwell."

On shaky legs, I forced my feet to move toward the door while my mind tried to wrap around the situation. "Thank you, Sam. I appreciate your willingness to give me a chance in spite of—" I choked on the words. "In spite of everything."

"Don't thank me. If I had my way, you'd be out on your ass, but Ansel made it a condition of the acquisition."

"Are you kidding me?" Anger prickled through my veins. He clasped his hands on the desk, a smug curl to the corners of his mouth. "You put me through this—this inter-rogation just for the hell of it?" I sputtered.

"Oh, no. I assure you I meant every word of it." He was toying with me, and judging by his smirk, enjoying it entirely too much. A dozen uncharitable insults bubbled to my lips, most of them containing colorful profanity. If it had been anyone else, anyone but him, I would've given him the dressing down of his life. Deep down, I knew I deserved his punishment. I choked back the words and bit my lower lip to hold them in. "Ansel seems to think highly of you. God knows why." His declaration stung almost as much as his next request. "I'd appreciate it if you called me Mr. Seaforth after this. Only my friends call me Sam. No one knows about our past, and I'd like to keep it that way." And then he went in for the kill. "You'll report to me tomorrow morning. You'll be working directly with me. If I can't get rid of you, the least I can do is make your life a living hell for the next six months."

The door thudded shut behind me. Curious employees stared over cubicle walls. Lifting my chin, I retraced my steps to my office and sank into my chair, shell-shocked. I'd gone into Sam's office concerned about my future and had come out more fearful than ever. By securing my job, Ansel had locked me into a six-month contract with the devil.

4

DAKOTA - THEN

THE LIMOUSINE turned down a dirt road at the edge of town and stopped beside a forest thick with aged trees and heavy underbrush. An eight-foot chain link fence topped by razor wire—the kind around prisons—contained the woods. Every ten feet or so, a sign declared *Private Property—No Trespassing*. Whatever this fence contained must be pretty special or dangerous.

Under normal circumstances, the remote location would have triggered immediate apprehension. A glance at Sam's face reassured me. Although I didn't really know him, I knew of him. My mother always spoke highly of him, and he seemed innocuous enough, his wavy hair spilling over his forehead, features relaxed. I patted the prepaid cellphone in my pocket, for emergencies only at my mother's insistence. Rockwell, the driver, opened the door for us and provided a second source of reassurance. I recognized his face from my visits to the mansion. Our eyes met, and I frowned, fearing he would tell my mother. He gave me a reassuring wink, implying his secrecy.

"Um, tell me again why we're out here?" I swept a wary gaze around us. Born and raised in the city, I preferred concrete and steel to the flora and fauna of nature. A mosquito buzzed in my ear, and I waved it away.

"Come on. You'll see. It's really cool." Samuel headed toward the fence. He pulled a section of chain link away from its supporting post to reveal a slit large enough for us to squeeze through.

"Aren't you afraid of trespassing?" I asked.

He held back the fence with one hand and offered the other to help me pass. "It's hardly trespassing when your family owns the property. My dad put the signs up. He likes to hunt out here and stocks it with deer and stuff. Sometimes elk. He even had a few wild boar at one time."

A branch snapped in the undergrowth a few yards away. "What was that?" I froze and looked apprehensively from side to side, preparing to sprint back to the car. "Aren't boar dangerous?"

Laughter transformed his features, and I forgot to be frightened, transfixed by his wide grin, full lips, and perfect white teeth. "There aren't any here now. That was years ago. He's too obsessed with running his empire these days to do anything recreational."

He hadn't released my hand since we'd crossed through the fence. His grip tightened around my fingers. The pad of his thumb swept across the back of my hand. Everything south of my tummy clenched at his warm, proprietary touch. Did he hold his girlfriend's hand like this? Did he even have a girlfriend? I'd never seen him with a girl or heard of him dating anyone from our school. He probably had a supermodel tucked in another city or some heiress from his daddy's country club.

"Dakota?"

I blushed, hoping my face didn't give away my growing infatuation. He didn't notice and walked ahead of me, pulling me along the narrow path. We emerged into a circular clearing. Sunlight shafted through the trees, heating my skin. I flattened a hand over my eyes to cut the glare and squeaked in surprise. An abandoned house stood in front of us, surreal and enchanting, brimming with mystery. Ivy clung to the brick walls and climbed the pillars of the porch. The paint had long ago peeled from the wood scrollwork trim, but the bones of the structure remained solid.

"Wow. What is this place?" I surged toward the house, pulling him with me. The scents of damp earth and azaleas drifted on the air around us, reminders of impending summer.

"It's the original Seaforth house. My great-great grandfather built it. When he made his fortune, he left it to my great grandfather, who erected the house I live in now." Samuel stopped walking to stare up at the three stories of brick in front of us. "They used this one for guests and stuff for a while, then finally they abandoned it altogether."

"Can we go inside?"

"Sure." Another one of Sam's slow smiles warmed me. He took the front steps two at a time, opened the front door, and swept a hand to invite me inside.

The house was empty and smelled musty. A wide staircase swept through the foyer and curved to the second-floor landing. Remnants of former grandeur lingered among the hardwood floors and plaster cornices. Faded wallpaper peeled from the walls. I trailed a finger over the newel post at the foot of the stairs while Samuel watched from the center of the room. The weight of his gaze followed me as I peered in doors and hallways.

It wasn't a big house. The rooms were small, but the

ceilings stretched high above our heads, giving the illusion of space. In its day, it must have been a grand place, and I said as much to Samuel.

"Why would they leave a place like this?" I asked, bewildered by the concept.

Samuel shrugged. "Too expensive to add plumbing and electricity. And they wanted something bigger. Something to show off their wealth."

"Where did your family's money come from anyway?" I'd heard stories about the Seaforth wealth, tales of coal-mines and oil wells.

"My great-great-great grandfather started out as a black-smith, but he had bigger ideas. He scraped together some money and bought land. He found coal on one of his prop-erties and opened up a mine, working alongside his employ-ees. He was a self-made man."

The pride in his voice lifted him another notch in my esteem. I had a picture in my mind of someone who resem-bled Sam, sweating over an anvil, clawing out an empire from coal and iron. "That's pretty impressive. I had no idea."

We'd circled the ground floor and arrived back at the staircase. I stood on the lower step, which put me at eye level with Samuel. He stopped in front of me, inches away, and met my gaze. Something alive and pulsating zinged between us, hitting me like a thunderbolt deep in my belly, deeper between my legs. His focus dipped to my lips. For a second, I forgot to breathe, a situation made direr when he wrapped one of my escaped curls around his finger and tugged. Our smiles collided. We both looked away then back again.

"Why do you come here?" I followed him out the front door. We sat side by side on the concrete steps of the front porch, shoulders touching. "I thought you were going to take me to some swanky club or something."

"I like it here. It's quiet. Peaceful." His chest lifted and fell with a soft sigh. "It feels more like home than my house." He cast a sideways glance in my direction. "Someday—when I inherit this place—I'm going to restore it."

"I think that's a great idea. Like putting your own stamp on your family's legacy."

Sitting on the dilapidated porch together, it was hard to visualize him as the heir to a fortune. He lounged back on his elbows, long legs stretched in front of him, crossed at the ankles. A light breeze ruffled his hair. The scent of his cologne, spicy and clean, wafted around me.

"So what's it like? Being rich, I mean. Having your every heart's desire." I said this teasingly, intending to lighten his somber mood, but he didn't smile. Instead, he cocked his head to one side while he considered his answer.

"It doesn't suck," he replied. "But it's a little like eating ice cream every day for every meal. At first you think it's great, but after a while you start to get sick of it and all you can think about is a ham sandwich and some chips."

"Is that what you want? A ham sandwich?" It was hard to believe when he could have anything and everything he wanted. The disparity of our lives wallowed between us. While my family scrimped and saved to afford basic needs, his family spent summers in Europe and organized fundraisers for people like me. "You can have anything in the world and you choose a ham sandwich? Not caviar or lobster?"

"I'm allergic to shellfish," he deadpanned and bumped my shoulder with his. "What would you have?"

"I'd buy my mom a house," I answered without hesitation. I'd fantasized about freeing her life from debt and worry. The answer sprang to my lips. "Pay off all her loans."

"Nothing for yourself?" Samuel cocked his head, eyes narrowing in disbelief, as if I'd spoken a foreign language. I shook my head. "Not a new car or clothes or a vacation?"

"I don't need anything." I nudged his shoe with my toe. "Just a roof over my head and clothes on my back."

"Me too."

When silence stretched between us once more, I glanced up at him. His gaze searched my face, stripping me bare to my bones. An unfamiliar thickness constricted my throat. What was he looking for? One of his hands lifted to touch my chin. The pad of his thumb stroked across my bottom lip. His eyes darkened. My heart kicked against my ribs as he leaned forward, drawing my body toward his by sheer magnetism.

He tasted of mint, the pressure of his lips soft and chaste against mine. The light contact disoriented my thoughts until I lost track of right and wrong, up and down. His hand cupped my cheek, fingers warm, the way one would touch something precious and fragile. When he pulled back, a small sigh escaped me, half moan, half needy. I'd kissed a dozen other boys, but none of them had ever affected me this way.

"What was that for?" I asked, my voice a whisper.

"I wanted to see if you taste as sweet as you look."

"Am I a ham sandwich?" I asked then blushed at the idiotic words.

He laughed, the sound warm and genuine. "All this talk about food is making me hungry. You want to grab something to eat?" He stood and extended his hand to me. I took it, curling my fingers through his, and he pulled me to my feet. We walked back to the limo. He didn't release my hand, and I didn't mind.

DAKOTA - NOW

*I*F I can't get rid of you, the least I can do is make your life a living hell for the next six months. Sam's parting words stuck with me all the way home. I decided to walk instead of taking the bus and use the time to work off a little of the turmoil swirling inside me. It didn't help.

Ten years ago, I'd done a despicable thing. Sam had married me because he loved me and had given up his inheritance to do so. Two years later, Sam's father had offered me a million dollars to divorce his precious only son, the heir to his kingdom. I'd taken the money, packed my bags, and left the love of my life without so much as a good-bye. A stringent set of guidelines, set forth by Sam's father, had accompanied the payoff. The most painful being no contact with Sam. Mr. Seaforth wanted me to leave without explanation or warning. His intention had been to make Sam hate me, and judging by the tension in Sam's jaw today, he'd been successful.

The sight of those seven figures in my bank account had turned my stomach. I'd refused to spend the money on myself. Instead, I'd used it to fund my mother's heart surgery and kept my brother out of jail on numerous occasions. I'd used the balance to purchase a condo so Mom would have a place to live in her retirement. No matter how dirty it had felt to take the money, it had gone to good use. Precious little comfort it was to me now.

A few tears escaped and slid down my cheeks. I let them fall. The sidewalk beneath my feet blurred and wavered. The heel of my shoe caught in a crack, and my ankle rolled to the side with a painful pop.

I groaned and tried to place some weight on the injured foot. A shard of pain rocketed up my calf. I hopped to lean against the doorway of Jameson's Pub. I'd been inside a few times, although my taste went toward edgier, more eclectic clubs. I shuffled inside, limping and wincing with each step.

It took a second for my eyes to adjust after the brilliant glare of sunlight outside. Dark wood, gleaming brass, and Old World ambience closed in around me. The low hum of civilized conversation hung in the air. Once I'd gathered my bearings, I took a seat at the closest table and propped my leg on a chair to survey the damage.

"Wow. That's impressive." A deep male voice floated down to me. I followed the stretch of black trousers and starched white dress shirt to the twinkling brown eyes of the bartender, Jack.

"Thanks," I said. "It's a talent."

"Want some ice for that?"

"Would you mind?" My ankle was already swelling, the skin turning an ominous shade of lavender.

Jack returned with a plastic baggy filled with ice. He wrapped a towel around it and squatted beside me before placing it gently over the injury. "I brought you a shot of whiskey. On the house." His fingers lingered on my bare ankle. The curling lines of a tattoo peeked from beneath the cuff of his shirt. "You look like you need it."

"Thanks." I tossed the shot down, enjoying the burn and warmth. "I'll have ten more."

He laughed, and two deep dimples winked from his cheeks. Despite the pain of my ankle and inner turmoil over Samuel, I couldn't help but notice the glossy spill of brown hair over Jack's shoulders or the way his lips curled at the corners like question marks. I recognized the interest in his eyes. A year ago, six months ago—hell, a week ago—I would've been all over this hunk of man candy. I'd been through dozens of one-night stands in an effort to erase Sam's memory. Now that Samuel was back in my life, the idea of sleeping with another man knotted my insides, as if I'd be cheating on him. The irony of my loyalty to a man who hated me only added to my confusion. I was seriously messed up.

"On second thought, maybe I'll just call a cab and head home."

"Are you sure? I'll be off work in about an hour." He stood, towering over me, one eyebrow quirked in question. "I could take you home then."

"Yes, I'm sure, but thanks anyway."

He shrugged, unoffended. We'd hooked up once before —a drunken, impromptu fuck in the pub's restroom. Jack understood and respected the art of casual sex. Judging by the number of female eyes watching us, he'd have no problem finding another companion.

"I'll call a cab for you." He paused, reached into his pants pocket, and pulled out a business card. "Hey, I'm working at my uncle's club this weekend. Come by and see me. Bring your girlfriends."

I took the card and shoved it into my purse without

looking at it. After my day, the weekend seemed a century away. I was more concerned about surviving the rest of the evening without the heady pressure of tomorrow. Another day with Samuel. A flurry of butterfly wings beat inside me at the thought.

"I'll think about it," I said.

The cab dropped me in front of the limestone apartment building and was gone before I limped to the entrance. The pain in my ankle had receded to a dull throb but started up again once I reached the elevator. Needless to say, I was in a pretty foul mood by the time I entered my apartment to find my brother, Crockett, sprawled on the sofa and the entire place in shambles.

Don't get me wrong. I loved Crockett. The things I'd done for him should prove it, but after ten years of lying for him, fixing his problems, and sacrificing my life for his, my patience was worn thin. The sight of him in his underwear at six-thirty in the evening on a Monday didn't help.

"Dude? What the fuck?" I prodded him with a reluctant finger. He rolled onto his back, throwing an arm over his eyes, and stirred the odors of cigarettes and beer. I coughed and waved a hand in front of my face. "You stink. Get off my couch."

"Love you, too," he mumbled. One eyelid cracked to a slit, exposing a blue iris, then slid shut, overwhelmed by the sight of me.

"I'm serious, Crockett." I shoved his shoulder, hard enough to make him grunt. "I've had a day." As if to remind me, my ankle cried out, throbbing with every beat of my heart. "What are you doing here anyway?"

With a groan, I sank into the club chair and propped my

foot on the ottoman. Crockett sat up and scrubbed his face with both hands, palms rasping over his unshaven cheeks and jaw. We didn't look much alike, existing on opposite ends of the spectrum. He'd shaved his dark hair into a Mohawk. The gelled ends drooped limply over his forehead and ears. Random tattoos covered his chest. Not the sexy kind. These were angry and crude jailhouse tats, the lines blurred and uneven.

"I got fired."

"Again? Are you kidding me?" Anger and frustration bubbled up inside me. My nerves were already stretched to the breaking point, and I yearned for someone to take it out on.

"Don't start with me, Kota." He held up a hand to ward off the tirade forming on my lips. "It's just temporary. I've already got a line on something else."

A line. I tried to pretend I didn't know what those words meant, but years of experience had taught me what to expect. Drugs. Fencing stolen merchandise. Running bets for bookies. Crockett lived on a side of the law I tried hard to avoid.

"I went out on a limb to get you that job. You barely made it two weeks." I leaned my head against the back of the chair. Exhaustion shimmered through my body, weighting my eyelids. "If you don't have a job, you'll violate your probation and go back to jail. You know that, right?"

"Yeah, yeah. I know."

From behind closed eyelids, I heard the flick of a lighter, the sizzle of the flame as it touched the end of his cigarette, and the hiss of his breath when he inhaled. "You can't smoke in here. How many times do I have to tell you?"

His footsteps shuffled across the room to the window. I heard him lift the sash. A light breeze cooled my skin, refreshing after the emotional heat of the day. He sighed, the frustration softening my heart a little. "I'm sorry, kiddo. I promise I'll get something tomorrow."

Crockett's broken promises filled the silence between us. We both knew he wouldn't get a job, but we were stuck in an endless cycle of failure and redemption.

"I saw Samuel today." The confession escaped haltingly, but I had to tell someone, someone who knew the situation and wouldn't judge me for it.

"Really? No shit?" His tone held the smallest note of sympathy, and I clung to it with the desperation of a drowning woman on a life raft in the middle of the ocean.

"He's my new boss. He bought the company, I guess."

"Gee. Sucks for you." He sank back onto the sofa. I heard the cushions compress beneath his weight. "How is old Sam anyway?"

"Fine. Different," I said, unable to put all my thoughts into something as insubstantial as words. "Pissed."

"Yeah? I bet. That family always could hold a grudge."

Crockett left, and I retreated to my bedroom. For the first time in a long time, I cried myself to sleep. Betrayal and heartbreak haunted my dreams. I'd thought my life had ended when Samuel and I had divorced. With time, I'd made a new life and shoved the pain into the back of mind. I had healed, or so I thought until I saw Samuel. As it turned out, the hole in my heart was still there.

DAKOTA - NOW

B Y THE next morning, my ankle felt better but every muscle and nerve in my body vibrated with tension. I entered the building with my shoulders hunched around my neck and a furrow between my brows. As the elevator ascended to the thirty-seventh floor, my stomach began to churn with apprehension. The doors opened with a quiet *shoosh*, and I stepped into the reception area. Sadie took one look at my face and turned an odd shade of gray.

"Mr. Seaforth wants to see you right away," she said, voice quavering.

"I'm just going to put my things in my office first," I said, breezing by. "Tell him I'll be right there."

"Um, that's the thing." She dropped her gaze to the desk. "It's not your office anymore. He gave it to Dahlia."

I halted then retraced my steps to her desk. She studied the pen in her trembling hands with rapt fascination. "I'm sorry. What did you say?"

Her words tumbled out in a rush. "He had your things

moved to the cubicle outside his office last night. He said he needed you where he could keep an eye on you."

Rage, embarrassment, and disbelief flooded through me. It wasn't Sadie's fault, but I glared at her anyway. The office fell quiet as I stomped down the hall, heedless of my bum ankle. The rapid tattoo of my steps echoed off the tiled floor. Valerie jumped to her feet, hands waving to stop me. I pushed past her and threw open the door to Sam's office. He was standing near the windows and turned to face me when I entered, a menacing scowl darkening his brow.

"What the hell, Samuel?" I hissed through my clenched jaw. "You threw me out of my office? Is this how it's going to go?"

He had been on the phone when I interrupted. He clicked off the call and regarded me with bland amusement. I tensed as he walked toward me then passed to close the door in the faces of my curious coworkers. His cool silence only served to fuel my indignation.

"Sit down, Ms. Atwell." He gestured to a chair as he returned to the desk. When I didn't sit, his eyes narrowed. I crossed my arms over my chest. He remained standing, legs braced as if I might suddenly rush him.

"I understand that you hate me, Samuel. I get it, and I don't blame you, but it doesn't give you the right to toss me out of my office—"

"I can do anything I want, Ms. Atwell. Do I need to remind you that it's my company now and my office?" He mirrored my defensive stance.

"I worked hard for that office," I said, feeling my blood pressure rise. "And I will continue to work just as hard for you, but it's not fair." As soon as the childish words left my mouth, I wished I could suck them back in.

"Do you want to know what's not fair? Having your

wife leave you like a thief in the night without so much as a goodbye. Learning she loved your father's money more than she loved you. That's not fair, Dakota." He sank into his chair and kicked back. The blood in my veins turned to ice. He knew about the money. Had his father told him? Of course he had. Mr. Seaforth had wanted me out of Sam's life, and nothing would cement the transaction more than Sam's hatred.

"It was never about the money." Bile churned in my stomach. "If you'd let me explain—"

"I have no interest in your explanations. I owe you nothing. Less than nothing. And that's what you'll get from me." Although his words held conviction, his tone remained impassive. "So suck it up, sweet pea. Welcome to the big leagues."

The use of his pet name for me renewed my distress. We stared at each other while I tried to regroup my composure. The nickname conjured up visions of snuggling together in bed on rainy Sunday mornings and eating Chinese food from paper cartons in the kitchen of our shitty off-campus apartment. We'd been in love then, not mortal enemies. The memory closed my throat, and I made a small strangled sound. My irritation dissipated, replaced by bittersweet nostalgia.

"I'm sorry. You're right." I inhaled deeply, renewing my resolve to get through this charade. This was his game. His rules. "Whatever you need, I'll do it."

My answer seemed to take him by surprise. He pushed back in his chair and cocked his head. The gesture was familiar and foreign at the same time. After a slow blink, he said, "Great. Then let's get to work. I'm going to need your help with some things."

SAMUEL - NOW

DAKOTA DROPPED an armload of reports on the conference room table Tuesday and stood in front of me, waiting for her next assignment. By the frown on her face, she didn't care much for the tasks I'd given her. Over the course of the day, I'd sent her out for coffee to the farthest location in the city and had her pick up my dry cleaning. To cap the afternoon, I'd requested lunch from a sandwich shop I knew didn't deliver, then sent her back twice to change my order. Menial tasks more suited for an entry-level assistant than the Project Acquisitions Director. In fact, I'd spent more time inventing "punishments" for her than I'd spent going over the company information. I'd waited ten long years for my revenge, and I intended to enjoy every minute of it.

Our encounter at the coffee shop had caught me off guard. I'd been prepared to meet her. I hadn't been prepared to find her so damned attractive. What really pissed me off was how completely fuckable she looked. A straight blue skirt hit her mid-thigh, showing toned legs, and a tight white blouse covered breasts larger and perkier than I remembered.

Her frustrated sigh brought a smile to my lips. I covered it with a scowl and dropped my gaze to the report in my hand. Data swam across the pages in a nonsensical blur. I'd been preparing for this merger over the past six months. I already knew everything I needed to know about the company. In truth? I was just fucking with her. It was petty, I knew. I couldn't help myself.

"Is there anything else I can get you?" she asked after I'd left her standing there for another couple of minutes. When I didn't answer, her eyes narrowed. "Shine your shoes, maybe? Or would you prefer some lemonade squeezed by tiny elves with lemons from the Enchanted Forest?"

"Did you say something?" I lifted my gaze to find her staring at me with eyes the color of the Mediterranean Sea —not blue, not green, but some exotic mixture in the middle.

I'd forgotten about those eyes, the way they could reach down inside me and twist my guts with a flutter of lacy black lashes. They were my Kryptonite. I had to blink away from them and focus on the view outside the wall of windows to shake their hold. When I looked back to her, she'd gone pale and sank into a chair.

"Are you okay?" I might be petty and juvenile, but I wasn't a complete asshole. By the expression on her face, something was terribly wrong.

"I'm fine," she said in a thin voice. "I just need to sit for a minute. I'm feeling a little dizzy."

"Pregnant?" I asked and immediately regretted it.

Her expression twisted and her gaze dropped to her lap. Children had been a hot topic for us. I'd wanted lots and she'd wanted to wait, a point made moot by our divorce. "I twisted my ankle last night," she said. "And it hurts like a mother." As she spoke, she lifted her foot and propped it on the empty chair between us. The ankle had turned a yellowish-purple, swollen to the size of a grapefruit.

"Jesus, Dakota." At the sight of her injury, my asshole persona slipped away, forgotten. Before she could protest, I lifted her foot from the chair and eased her shoe off. She winced. I dangled the stiletto in the air by one of the delicate straps. I had a quick mental image of Dakota in those shoes and nothing else. Always a sucker for a pretty girl, my traitorous groin tightened. "Maybe you should've worn more sensible shoes."

"I didn't realize I'd be walking all over town for the better part of the day," she huffed.

"You need to get some ice on this."

"I'll be fine." She moved to reclaim her foot, but I clamped a hand around her calf.

"Sit tight. I'll be right back." I stepped outside the office and shot orders at Valerie for an icepack and aspirin.

When I returned, her head rested against the back of the chair, eyes closed, and lips parted. A picture of her asleep on the sofa of our apartment, lashes fanned across her cheeks, hand curled beneath her chin, flashed through my memory. I used to love watching her sleep, tracing the lines of her upturned nose and the short bow of her upper lip with my fingers, holding my breath so I wouldn't wake her.

"Fuck," I muttered.

"What?" Her eyes fluttered open.

"Nothing. Here. Ibuprofen." I set the caplets on the table, alongside a glass of water. She eyed them warily. "Oh, for goodness sake. I'm not trying to poison you."

"Can you blame me?" she asked, but tossed the pills into her mouth and chased them down with a gulp of water.

"You're not getting off that easy," I replied, only half joking. "I need to keep you around so I can torture you."

I eased her foot from the chair and into my lap then placed the icepack on her ankle. Her foot weighed nothing in my hand, the bones small and fragile, flesh warm and firm. Pink polish tipped each of her delicate toes. I resisted the urge to run my hands over her arch, remembering how she loved a good foot massage.

"I couldn't get that lucky," she muttered. An expression of sadness shadowed her face and faded away as quickly as it came. Empathy squeezed my heart.

Oh, no. No, no, no. I would not feel sorry for her, no matter how bad or how sad her life might be. Whatever strife existed in her life had been her own doing. Karma was a bitch. And I hoped it bit her in the ass.

"You need to see a doctor." I released her foot and pushed my chair to a safe distance where I could no longer feel her body heat or smell her perfume. What was it? Something sweet and citrusy, clean but spicy. I drew in a second, longer sniff to better analyze the scent.

"If I see a doctor, he'll just put me off work and my new boss won't like it."

"He must be a dick," I replied.

"He's not," she said. "He's a very nice man and a friend of my mother's. He's been our family doctor for years."

One corner of my mouth tugged up, and I bit back the smile. Such a smart ass, my little Dakota. "I meant your boss."

"Oh. I don't know about him. He didn't used to be." The weight of her gaze drew my eyes to hers. "I thought he was a great person once. Maybe he still is underneath all his ass-hat tendencies." She gave me a one-shouldered shrug.

This revelation sat me back in my chair while I scanned her face to judge the sincerity in her expression. I'd been nothing but mean to her. Cold. Aloof. Unyielding. I wanted her to hate me the way I hated her. Yet, she continued to hold on to the boy I'd once been instead of the man I'd become. The walls of my chest constricted until I had to look away and calm my racing pulse. She always saw me for who I was and not what I represented. It was what had drawn me to her in the first place all those years ago.

"Take a few minutes and get yourself together." I stood and straightened my tie, disconnecting my gaze from hers. "I need you to go through all the files in my office and sort them by date and company." She sighed through her nose, an exasperated snort that would've been cute on any other female. "Before tomorrow." With those parting words, I turned and headed toward the door. "I'll be out the rest of the day."

I didn't really have anywhere to go, but I couldn't spend another minute in close confines with her. My lingering attraction to her pissed me off. In my mind, I'd turned her into a three-eyed troll with warts. I didn't expect to find a doe-eyed, voluptuous knockout with a shrewd intellect. At the curb in front of the building, I passed a hand over my face and waited for Rockwell. I needed to get over this or it was going to be a very long six months.

SAMUEL - THEN

INSIDE THE limo, Dakota sat on the gray leather seat across from me. I tried not to stare at the way the hem of her skirt rode up a little too high on her thigh. She wore the requisite school uniform—plain white blouse with a black tie, navy blue skirt, and white knee socks. The ambiguous cut of the clothing hid most of her curves, but the smooth stretch of her legs captured my eighteen-year-old mind. Catching the trajectory of my gaze, she frowned and tugged her skirt down to her knees.

I'd started offering her a ride home after school. She always had us drop her a few blocks from her house. I wasn't quite sure why. Maybe she didn't want her friends or parents to know about us. Maybe she still felt the disparity of our social classes. All I knew was that I enjoyed her company, and I didn't give a shit where she lived or who her mother was. She didn't ask anything of me or use me for my money. The few times I'd tried to buy her something, she'd tossed my debit card back at me. In a world where everyone wanted something, it was refreshing behavior.

On this particular afternoon, we were going back to my

house. My mother was having another one of her insuffer-able dinner parties and needed help with the setup. The idea of Dakota in my house had me oddly excited. Although I was pretty sure Mother wouldn't approve of transporting hired help in the limousine, I used it as an excuse to keep Dakota as a captive audience for the duration of the thirty-minute ride.

I broke the silence with a question that had nagged me for weeks. "Seaforth is an expensive school. How can your family afford for you to go there?"

Color rushed into her cheeks. It started as a pale pink at her collarbone and blossomed into rose red. She had the prettiest skin, translucent and smooth. My fingers itched with the urge to stroke the column of her neck and feel the pulse beating at the curve of her jaw.

"I'm sorry. I didn't mean to embarrass you." Too late, I realized my gaffe and felt the gap widen between our socio-economic standings.

"It's a fair question." She turned her gaze from the window to meet mine and smiled. Her smiles were rare, and the sight of even one warmed my insides in a way that reminded me of sunshine after a rainstorm. "I got a scholarship."

"So you're a brainiac."

She shrugged and brushed her hair back from her shoul-der. Usually she wore it in a ponytail, but today it hung in kinky spirals down her back. "Every year, your family offers assistance to public school students with exceptional skills. I applied last year and won," she said with a certain amount of pride in her voice.

"I knew it," I replied, captivated by the way the after-noon light shimmered in her eyes.

"Knew what?"

I had her full attention now. She turned her shoulders toward me, facing me fully, rewarding me with a full view of arched eyebrows, high cheekbones, and a small, pouty mouth.

"That you were exceptional."

DAKOTA - NOW

WITH A sigh of resignation, I eyed the endless files in front of me and recognized the task for what it was—retribution. Most of the documents deserved to be shredded. They were out of date and obsolete. The majority of the information existed online. But if he wanted me to sort through the junk, then sort I would. If only to show my determination and willingness to make this work.

Hours passed. The other employees powered down their computers and made their way to the elevators. The fluorescent lights of the office extinguished, and the low murmur of voices dissipated until I was left alone with massive stacks of paper and my dangerous thoughts. The more I worked, the more painful memories returned. While the sun lowered in the sky outside, my spirits lowered inside the office. Samuel hated me. I hated myself even more. It was going to be a long six months.

The office door opened, startling me from introspection. I squeaked and dropped a document folder, spilling pages over the plush carpet. Samuel looked up from the threshold, his features displaying momentary shock before schooling into cool ambivalence. My pulse skipped a beat. Attraction sparked inside me, while my intellect steeled for battle.

"You're still here." His deep, rich voice held a note of flat disappointment.

My spirits sank another notch, and my shoulders slumped a little. "Uh, yes. You said to have this done today, and I'm not finished yet." I scanned the stacks of untouched papers. "There's enough work here to keep me busy for a week."

He tugged his tie loose and unbuttoned the collar of his shirt then sank into his chair, his movements uncoordinated and choppy. His gaze rested on me. Although his features remained expressionless, his eyes were turbulent, assessing, and angry. The chair squealed in protest as he leaned back, perilously close to tipping, and propped his feet on the desk. The room filled with his masculinity and the scent of liquor. I tried not to notice the way his shirt stretched over his abs or the bunch of his trousers over his hips.

"You're drunk." Despite my best efforts, I sounded like an accusing wife.

"I'm shit-faced." He scratched his chin, the stubble of his beard rasping against his palm.

"Must be a personal problem. Have you thought about counseling?"

"Been there, done that."

The matter-of-fact honesty in his tone twisted my guts. Had I driven him to psychiatric intervention? The idea of wrecking this beautiful man hurt me more than I cared to admit. I covered it with anger. "Sounds like you need some more."

"More working. Less talking," he slurred. "Don't mind

me. I'm just going to sit here and think about all the ways you've fucked me over."

I'd been gathering up the scattered documents and stopped short at his words. With slow, deliberate movements, I straightened and stalked to his side. I dropped the folder onto the desk and scowled down at him. A dark growth of afternoon beard shaded his cheeks and jaws. He smelled of bourbon and cigars. The Samuel I knew—my Samuel—never drank or smoked. He abhorred self-destructive behavior. This bleary-eyed man seemed the antithesis of that boy.

"I'll save you the trouble," I said. "I'm a lying, deceitful bitch who broke your heart for a few bucks. Did I leave anything out?"

My heart lurched as he rose to his feet and stared down his nose at me. A muscle ticked in his jaw. His hand captured my chin and held it, forcing my gaze up to his. The pad of his thumb stroked over my lower lip in a gesture all too gut-wrenchingly familiar but lacking its former gentleness. When his eyes dipped to my lips, every fiber in my being trembled. *Kiss me.* No, wait. What was I thinking? Damn. Now I couldn't think of anything but how he would taste, the slide of his tongue over mine, the heat of his sigh against my mouth, how good it had been between us. My fingers curled in rebellion, wanting to fist in his hair.

"You have no idea, Dakota," he said in a hoarse voice. Was it my imagination, or had his voice gotten deeper, throatier?

"Then tell me, Samuel. Let's get it all out on the table. I can't take six months of this."

His hand slid from my jaw, wrapping around the column of my neck. I felt the power in his grip, barely leashed and dying to escape. Would he strangle me if he could? My pulse fluttered beneath his thumb. Our eyes met, and a sense of calm descended over me. Somewhere inside this raging man existed the boy I'd married, the one I'd loved, the one who'd loved me back.

"I'd like to wring your pretty little neck. Shake the life out of you." Eyes closed, he ran the tip of his nose alongside mine, not touching me but close enough to raise all the tiny hairs on my skin. "Throw you over my knee and spank your sweet round ass." His free hand rested on the small of my back. It drifted down to squeeze a handful of the body part in question. The span of his chest lifted and fell with a deep inhale. "Or maybe I'll just bend you over this desk and fuck you into oblivion."

I'll take fucking, please. The space between my legs developed a sweet ache. I had a quick mental image of my cheek pressed against the cool wood of the desk, his hands sliding my skirt up over my bare bottom, and his legs spreading mine wide. I dragged in a frustrated breath. "Maybe you should."

"Which one?" He drew back enough to give me a glimpse of the brown flecks in his irises, edged by thick, dark lashes.

I placed a hand on his chest to push him away but got lost in the sensation of my first contact with him. Beneath my palm, his chest was warm and hard. His heart beat against my touch, strong, vital, and insistent.

"Strangle me. Spank me. Fuck me." The last words left my lips on a whisper, but he heard them. His eyes narrowed.

"It was always good between us, wasn't it?" His voice cracked on the question, as if he was parched. "The sex?"

"It was better than good." That wasn't an exaggeration. In my mind, I'd built it up to be epic.

"So you remember?" he asked, searching my eyes.

I nodded. How could I forget? For the first six months of our marriage, we'd barely left the bedroom except to work and eat. We'd had sex on every horizontal surface and some of the vertical ones.

Without releasing me, he walked me backward until my butt hit the edge of his desk. The pressure of the hand on my neck increased, pushing me down until I reclined on my back. My breath stuttered in short pants. He spread my thighs, pushing my skirt up to my hips. One hand lifted my knee to his waist. Right or wrong, I wanted him. The desk was cold and hard beneath me. The man between my legs was also hard, but more heated and more unforgiving.

Samuel dragged his gaze to my lips. His shoulders blocked out the sight of everything beyond him. The fabric of his shirt pulled taut over his biceps. His hand slid from my neck, over my chest, and came to rest on the placket of my blouse. I heard the rending of silk and the ping of buttons on the floor as he ripped the shirt open to my waist and yanked the cup of my bra down. His fingers sought my breast. My skin buzzed beneath his touch, the nipple tightening into a tense peak.

"Go ahead. Do it," I taunted. He answered by pressing his cock against my panties, the long, rigid length of it obvious despite the layers of cloth between us. "You know you want to."

His hand released my knee. I heard the jingle of his belt buckle, followed by the growl of his zipper. Unable to look anywhere but up, I focused on his eyes, vibrant and stormy. Our harsh breathing shattered the silence. The tension in his jaw renewed the ache between my legs. He might hate me, but he wanted me more. I arched up, dying to feel him inside me. Not because he loved me, but to punish me for everything I'd done to him. I wanted him to take all the frustration, resentment, and anger out on my body, to fuck me until nothing remained but the empty shell of the traitorous woman I'd become.

Suddenly, he pushed away from me, leaving my legs dangling over the desk edge, and ran a hand through his hair. He turned his back and spoke in a rough, cold voice. "You're not worth it."

"What?" The absence of his body heat sent a shiver through me. I sat up and clutched the edges of my blouse over my breasts. Humiliation burned in my cheeks, chased away the lust, and left me with an aching emptiness. I'd been hurt before, but nothing ever hurt like those four words. I already felt unworthy. The cold steel in his gaze cemented the truth of it.

"Get out." His tone held a world of implications. His shoulders hunched as he tucked his shirt into his pants and did up the fly.

"But I'm not done with—" The protest died on my lips at the sight of his face. Brow furrowed, eyes narrowed, lips pressed into a thin, tight line.

"Just go, Dakota."

If he wanted to hurt me, he'd succeeded. I slid off the desk, forgetting about the pain in my ankle and the torn front of my blouse. Without a backward glance, I walked straight past him and out the door. Tears blurred my vision. I grabbed my purse from my cubicle, boarded the elevator, and rode to the lobby in a haze of humiliation.

DAKOTA - THEN

ON A rainy Saturday afternoon, I sat in the family dining room, surrounded by a plethora of utensils. There were items I'd never had a need to use, and some I couldn't identify. Mrs. Seaforth breezed in and out of the room a dozen times while I worked. She was a tall, willowy woman with a pinched mouth and eyes the same shade of green as Sam's. On the last visit, she paused at my elbow to inspect my work.

Once each spring, Mrs. Seaforth threw a charity ball at the mansion. It was a decadent extravaganza for which my mother prepared months in advance. She labored over recipes and presentations, working with Mrs. Seaforth to devise the perfect menu. Gardeners tidied the landscaping. Extra help came in to clean the house. Crockett did small odd jobs around the property. I spent hours polishing the silver table service. It was boring work but provided extra cash above the paltry allowance my parents gave me.

Sam and I were both eighteen now. Graduation and college loomed in front of us, mere weeks away. He would be off to Princeton, while I had a scholarship to the local university. Neither of us had mentioned the upcoming separation or what it might mean for our relationship. The idea of losing him so soon after finding him made my chest ache, and my thoughts turn gray.

"Do be careful, Dakota." Mrs. Seaforth's cultured voice held a note of disapproval. "This silver has been in my family since before the Revolutionary War, and it's worth a fortune."

"Don't worry. I'll be very careful," I replied, too lost in hazy daydreams about Sam to take offense at her patronizing tone.

"Of course you will, dear." She patted my shoulder, her gaze catching her reflection in the gilt-framed mirror above my head. She turned her head from left to right, assessing her image. "And I will do an inventory when you're done."

"As well you should," I replied, cheerfully pretending to miss the insult. Once she'd left the room, I ran an admiring finger over the butter knife in my hand. Intricate curls and flowers adorned the handle. It was truly remarkable. Not for the first time, I wondered what it would be like to own something so precious and valuable. My musings were interrupted by a low, masculine voice in my ear.

"What are you doing?" Samuel leaned over the back of my chair, his lips so close I felt the buzz of his lips on my neck. He pressed a kiss on my pulse point, raising gooseflesh across my shoulder.

"I'm working. Go away." I gave him a playful shove, propelling him back a step. A wave of giddiness swept over me, the way it did every time I saw him now. Just being in the same room with him elicited tingles of excitement in my deepest recesses.

"Let's go." He jingled a set of car keys on a leather fob in front of my nose.

"Your car? You got it back?" He nodded, eyes shining with adventure. Nothing pleased me more than seeing him happy.

"No more Rockwell." He removed the knife from my hand and curled his fingers around mine, tugging me to stand next to him. "I want to take you for a ride before it starts raining again."

"But your mother?" I gestured to the table and the mountain of silver to be polished.

"We'll be quick," he promised and touched the tip of my nose with his forefinger. "She won't even know you're gone. Don't say no."

How could I ever deny him anything when he looked at me with those grass-green eyes full of promise? We'd gone from casual acquaintances to constant companions in the space of a few months. He waited for me at my locker between classes and gave me a ride home in the limo after school. After the first few times, I gave up the pretense of hiding my address and let him take me to my doorstep. Often times, he kissed me goodbye when no one was watching. I lived for those kisses, and I lived for the time we spent together.

Samuel pressed the accelerator to the floor, and the car purred in response. It was a beautiful automobile, sleek and sexy, just like Samuel. I snuggled deeper into the soft leather seat and stared at his profile. He shot a sideways glance at me, full mouth curved into a smile, before down-shifting and easing into a curve. The sleeves of his sweater stretched tight over his biceps. His confidence sparked a new awareness inside me. He filled the car with his maleness. In contrast, I felt small and utterly feminine beside him.

"What?" he asked, shooting me another glance.

"Nothing," I said, a blush heating my cheeks.

"It's got to be something." He released the gearshift long enough to brush a finger over the side of my face.

"You're such a guy." I bit my lower lip to hold back a smile.

"Are you just now noticing?" he asked, arching an eyebrow. "I must not be doing it right."

"I thought you didn't care about material things, about stuff." I waved a hand to encompass the interior of the car.

"I said I don't care about the money," he corrected. "But in case you haven't noticed, this is a car, and cars are things of beauty. Works of art." The layers of richness in his voice set off a mini explosion inside me. His hand drifted down from my face to rest on top of my thigh. "Like you."

It had begun to rain. Fat drops pinged the windshield. He pulled onto a side street, and I recognized the park not far from the college campus. The rain began to fall harder. He parked the car beneath a spreading elm tree in a remote picnic area, where we were completely sheltered from view. Once he shut off the engine, we were left in insulated silence. A deep growl of thunder rolled in the distance.

"One, two, three, four..." I counted in a whisper and waited for the following flash of lightning.

"What are you doing?" I felt his curious gaze on me, sliding over me, warm and caressing.

"Counting the seconds between the thunder and the lightning." I winced as a second crack of thunder shattered the silence. "I hate storms. My dad always told me to count and then I'd know how far away the storm was."

"Does that work for you?" As he spoke, the hand on my

thigh drifted down my leg, his fingers curling to stroke the delicate skin behind my knee.

"Not really." The way he watched me, like I was something delicious to eat and he was starving, made my panties dampen.

"Are you scared now?" His voice deepened, impossibly deep for a boy. But he was a man, I reminded myself. In a few short months, school would be over, we'd graduate, and then head off to our respective colleges. Knowing everything between us might end gave our relationship an urgency.

"A little." I tore my gaze from him long enough to watch the rain pour in sheets over the windshield, obliterating everything from sight and secluding us in our own personal cocoon.

"Of me or the storm?" His hand tightened around my knee, the warmth of it searing my skin.

"Both," I whispered.

"Come here," he said, the words both a command and a request.

"Shouldn't we be getting back?" A tremor of excitement shook my hands. I clenched them in my lap to keep him from seeing. He was going to kiss me, and somehow I knew this time would be different. This time I wouldn't stop him or ask him to slow down or tear myself away like I had all the other times, because I wanted it. I wanted him in a way I'd never wanted anything before in my life.

"In a minute," he said, his voice lower still. "Come here, Kota."

I leaned toward him, drawn by his words, his voice, and the light in his eyes. I couldn't stay away even if I wanted to. He exuded magnetism, pulling me in like the moon orbiting the earth. When he shifted, I shifted.

"Samuel, I...we..." My voice broke when his lips brushed the corner of my mouth. It was the sweetest of touches. A fine layer of gooseflesh raised on my forearms. The next kiss landed beneath my ear. The next one on the curve of my neck. "Oh, um, okay."

"Dakota?" One of his fingers skimmed my collarbone, caught the edge of my sweater, and tugged it over my shoulder, taking my bra strap with it.

"Yes?" I closed my eyes and gave myself over to the sensation of his touch on my bare skin.

"Less talking. More kissing." With methodical thoroughness, he worked his way from my neck to my shoulder and down the slope of my breast. When his lips brushed my nipple for the first time ever, I slammed my thighs together, undone by the sudden jolt of aching pleasure in my sex.

He slipped an arm around my waist, lifting and sliding me over the console onto his lap. He was so powerful, so strong, and so safe. I let him move my legs until I straddled him. One of his hands left me long enough to adjust the seat back as far as it would go. For the briefest of seconds, it occurred to me he'd done this before, with some other girl. How else could he know exactly where my legs should go and how to move the seat to allow him room? Somehow it didn't matter. He was here. With me. And no one else mattered.

Neither of us were virgins. The way he pressed my hips down onto the hard ridge of his cock made it perfectly clear. I'd been with one boy in a misguided and awkward encounter the previous summer. The ensuing embarrassment had left me unwilling to try it again—until Samuel.

Everything about him suggested sex, sex, sex. I dreamed about him, doodled his name in the margins of my notebooks, and blushed every time someone mentioned him in casual conversation. He'd become the air I craved to survive. I wanted him to touch me, hold me, be inside me. Our previous encounters always ended with both of us frustrated and aching. He wanted to wait for sex until after I turned eighteen. All I wanted was him.

He seemed to be obsessed with me for reasons I never understood. We had little in common besides our sense of humor and loneliness. But when he looked at me, the way he was looking at me now, I felt desirable, admired, wanton.

"I want you, Dakota," he murmured in my ear. His big hands roamed restlessly up and down my thighs beneath my skirt, bunching it up toward my hips. I'd gone straight to his house after school and hadn't bothered to change.

"I want you too." I cupped his face in my hands, the stubble of his jaw tickling my palms. Our mouths found each other, snapping together, drawn like two magnets of opposing polarity. His tongue swept over mine, seeking and taking and tasting.

We kissed until the windows fogged over. We kissed until my lips felt swollen and tender. We kissed until every inch of my body ached with the need to have him inside me. When one of his fingers tested the edge of my white cotton panties, I didn't stop him. His finger slipped through my wetness, and a whimper of pure delight broke loose from my throat.

"Tell me this is real, Samuel," I whispered against his mouth. "I need to know I'm not dreaming this."

"It's real, baby," he said. He stroked me, up and down and in small circles, whipping my hormones into a frenzy of lust.

"I want you inside me." With my hands buried in his hair, I arched against him, needing to be closer.

"We need to be careful," he said, his voice rough with desire. "I don't have any condoms."

"I do. In my purse."

"You do?" He drew back, an expression of wary disbelief knotting his brow. "Should I be worried?"

"Mom," I answered. My mother, sensing the growing infatuation between us, had given a very impressive speech about abstinence and the responsibilities of parenthood. Then, in her practical manner, she'd given me a packet of condoms and asked if I needed to see a doctor.

"I love your mom," he sighed into my neck.

"Ew, gross," I scoffed.

He wasn't as practiced with the condom as I'd expected, so maybe my worries about other girls were unfounded. It took a good bit of maneuvering to get it on, given the size of the car's interior and the size of Samuel, but we managed. The second his erection nudged my entrance, my sex began to pulse and I lost all sense of time and space. I rocked against him, once more gripping his hair. He slid into me, slowly at first, his eyes locked with mine, then shoved all the way in with an expression so heart-wrenchingly intense that tears stung my eyes.

We moved together, awkwardly at first, and then settled into a rhythm. My thigh bumped the gearshift. I'd have a bruise there tomorrow. His knees thumped against the dashboard. It didn't matter. Ripples of heat flashed over my skin. The delicious fullness of his cock inside me, the way our bodies joined together, the slow and controlled thrust of his hips, kept me teetering on the brink of a powerful new sensation.

"You feel wonderful," he groaned. "So good. So tight." He jerked up, burying himself to the root. "I can't hold back anymore."

His declaration and the shift of his legs beneath me sent an undulating wave through my womb. My legs tensed. He slid his hands up my back, buried his face in my neck, and shuddered. For those few seconds, I owned him. When he cried out my name, I came and realized he owned me too.

By the time we returned to Sam's house, the rain had stopped, and orange and purple streaks layered across the sky. Time had gotten away from us. A small seed of foreboding took root in my chest. I pushed it away, too euphoric from our tryst to spoil the moment with worry. Samuel parked the car behind the garage. We ran to the back door of the house, holding hands, skipping over puddles, and laughing until we stepped into the mudroom.

Mr. Seaforth greeted us, a furrow between his brows and an intimidating downward curve to his mouth. His eyes roved over me. I lifted a self-conscious hand to smooth my hair. Samuel looked fine except for a few creases in his shirt. Me? Probably not so much. The smile on Sam's lips slid away at the sight of his father.

"Dakota, go to the kitchen. Your mother's waiting for you." Mr. Seaforth had a deep, quiet voice edged with steel. When he spoke, everyone listened. I was no exception. "Samuel, in my study."

My gaze bounced from Samuel to Mr. Seaforth and back again. Dread tightened my throat.

"It's okay," Samuel said. Our eyes met. He exuded calm. His lips smiled at me, but his eyes remained somber. "I'll see you at school tomorrow."

"Um, okay." I ducked my chin and headed to the kitchen, uncertain what to expect. Sam's hand brushed against me as I turned away, his little finger quirking around mine in a brief caress.

My mother stood in front of the giant pantry doors, hands on her hips and lips pursed in thought. She was a big woman, nearly six feet tall with platinum hair and hands the size of softball mitts. Her Swedish heritage showed in high-set cheekbones and fair skin, two traits I inherited from her. When I trudged into the kitchen, she greeted me with a cautious smile.

"And where have you been?" she asked, eyebrows lifting to her hairline.

"With Samuel," I said. "We went for a ride."

I slid onto a stool at the kitchen island to watch as my mother finished counting her supplies. It was a big industrial kitchen with granite countertops and stainless steel appliances. Copper pots and pans hung from hooks in the ceiling. The scent of fresh bread wafted from one of the ovens.

"Am I in trouble?" I asked when she didn't say anything more.

"What do you think?" She closed the pantry doors and turned to face me, placing her capable hands on the counter. "You were supposed to be working, not running around with the boss's son doing God knows what."

The heat of a thousand flames rushed into my cheeks. I looked down at my hands and chewed on the inside of my cheek. Mom had a way of shaming me with just a look. It was her superpower. She used it now.

"I know. I'm sorry. We only meant to be gone for a minute and we—we lost track of time."

"You like him, don't you?" She smiled and smoothed a hand over my hair, tucking a strand back behind my ear.

"I do." The hopefulness in my voice strained my throat.

"So do I. He's a good boy." She sighed and patted my cheek. "Go clean up the mess in the dining room. You'll owe Mrs. Seaforth an apology tomorrow. She's already gone to bed. Not feeling well this evening."

"I will." I smiled back at her, warmth replacing my earlier dread.

While she closed up the kitchen, I stole down the corridor toward the dining room. It was a rambling house with labyrinthine hallways, having rooms and additions built on by each generation of Seaforths. With thoughts of Samuel clouding my head, I made a wrong turn and ended up outside Mr. Seaforth's study. The sound of two raised voices halted my footsteps. The door was cracked open an inch. Golden lamplight spilled onto the patterned carpet of the hall.

"You can't tell me what to do," Samuel said. "I'm eighteen. I can do what I want."

"As long as you're under my roof, spending my money, you'll live by my rules," Mr. Seaforth thundered.

"It's always about the money with you." Sam's voice held the same steely edge as his father's.

"Try it and see how far you get without it," his father scoffed. "Do you think that girl gives a shit about you? I hate to break it to you, but without my money behind you, she'd never give you a second look."

"You think no one could care about me without the money? That I can't make it on my own?" By now, Sam's voice seethed with a fury I'd never heard before. "She's not like that, Dad. And neither am I."

"I'm not telling you to give her up, son. I'm just asking you to use a little restraint. You've got a bright future in front of you. Don't throw it all away on a pretty piece of ass. Especially not the cook's daughter. She's not worth it."

11

DAKOTA - NOW

IT TOOK all of my internal fortitude plus an extra twenty percent to walk through the revolving doors at work on Wednesday morning. Two days ago, I'd thrilled at the marble-and-glass lobby, the sight of Armani suits and Ferragamo shoes. Today, I felt like an imposter, a little girl playing dress-up. I'd come perilously close to throwing in the towel. In fact, I'd gone so far as to type out my resignation and attach it to an email addressed to Samuel Seaforth. It sat in my draft folder, waiting like an escape hatch on a sinking submarine, my lifeline to emotional rescue. Sheer stubbornness kept me from sending it.

He'd treated me like I was cheap and unworthy. Deep down I knew it wasn't him who'd made me feel that way. I already felt undeserving. His little power play only underscored the truth of my existence. Everything I had—my job, my mother's condo, Crockett's freedom—had come at a high price. For the longest time, I thought I'd paid the fee, but I was wrong. It was Samuel who'd paid the price, and I was the one who'd extracted it from him.

I sat in the chair at my cubicle and swallowed down the thick lump of self-loathing stuck in my throat. While my computer powered on, I shuffled through a dozen file folders dumped on my desk, each bearing a sticky note with instructions scrawled in Sam's slanting hand. I cast a furtive glance at his office, pulse beating erratically. The door was shut and the lights out. I exhaled in relief until I sighted Brian next to me.

"I see you've joined the general population like the rest of the lowly inmates," he said, plopping his ass on the desk at my elbow. "It seems you don't have this boss wrapped around your little finger like you did Ansel."

With all my nerves raw and exposed, I chose to ignore him rather than reply. I opened my work email and cringed at the ping of incoming messages. While Brian regarded me with unveiled amusement, I scanned through the subjects, deleting the junk and marking the important ones for follow-up. Even though Sam had demoted me, I still had customers who relied on me.

"I don't suppose you're still going to the Vandalia Charity Auction next month?" When I didn't answer, Brian waved a hand between my face and the computer screen, breaking my concentration. "Hello? Anybody in there?"

"No. I don't know. Maybe." I shoved his hand away. In all the turmoil surrounding Samuel and the takeover, I'd had little time to think about the event. Not that I had money to spend on the expensive auction items, but it was a good place to see and be seen by some of the city's biggest names. Before handing over the company, Ansel had purchased and distributed a dozen tickets to the executive staff.

"I just thought you might want to get rid of your ticket. I know somebody who needs one."

"Sure. I mean yes, I have a ticket." I dug blindly in my purse until my fingers found the ticket and held it in front of him about the same time my eyes landed on an email from Samuel. Brian reached for the ticket, and I snatched it back. "And no, you can't have it." I might not be going, but no way would I give it to him. Creeper.

He groaned. "Seriously? Come on."

"I said no." I nudged him off my desk with my elbow. "Shouldn't you be making sales calls or something?"

"Fine," he said. "But if you know someone who has an extra, let me know. Will you?"

In my head, I'd already dismissed him as I scanned over Sam's email with equal parts dread and anticipation.

I will be out of the office today. I've left a list of tasks for you with Valerie. I expect them to be completed when I return tomorrow morning. Get with her for any pertinent details you might need. Don't disappoint me.

That was it? Feeling curiously deflated, I sank back in my chair. Brian let out a low whistle, and I jerked, having forgotten him. With a seething glare, I minimized the email and turned to face him.

"Do you mind?" I snapped.

"That's cold. He really doesn't care for you. What did you do to him anyway?"

"Nothing." I grabbed a pen and notepad then stood, hoping to shoo Brian away.

"You've had to do something. He's got a reputation as a

pretty fair guy overall. Aside from the ruthless takeovers and dismantling companies and screwing other men's wives."

Brian's words stabbed me in the gut. "What do you mean by that?" The Samuel I knew would never do anything like that. Unless someone had crushed his heart. Someone like me.

"You mean you hadn't heard about it? He had an affair with his best friend's wife. It was all over the scandal rags last year." Brian shook his head. "The guy has some huge balls. It's true. Look it up."

I pushed past him and headed toward Valerie's desk. She glanced up at me with a smile and an expression of something I'd never seen from her before—sympathy. Brian trailed on my heels.

"You're disgusting. Go away." I returned Valerie's smile. "Samuel—I mean Mr. Seaforth—said he left a list for me with you."

"I do." She had an envelope in hand and offered it to me. "He said you were to get on it right away and that you would be out of the office the rest of the day."

"Great." Probably another plethora of tedious tasks, like finding silk sheets spun from Shangri La silkworms or something. With a supreme sense of dread, I ripped the envelope open and skimmed over the list. One item. *Go to the doctor.* I turned the page over. Blank. "That's it?"

"Yes. He was very adamant that you take care of it right away." Valerie raised her penciled eyebrows. "I wouldn't go against him, if I were you. He's very—" a dreamy film veiled her eyes, "—very alpha, isn't he?"

"Hmm... Well, okay." I folded the letter and shoved it back into the envelope, hiding it from the prying eyes of Brian, who was still hovering at my shoulder.

"What is it?" he asked.

"He said to start an audit of the expense accounts for all the marketing directors," I said.

Brian's footsteps scurried in the direction of his cubicle.

Valerie's smile broadened. "That's not what it says." She gave me a chastising shake of the head.

"Valerie, did you peek at the list?"

"I typed it up for him." The desk phone buzzed, and she turned to answer it with a professional, "Samuel Seaforth's office."

I waved goodbye and headed to the elevators, more confused than ever.

12

SAMUEL - NOW

UNABLE TO face Dakota on Wednesday, I invented a bevy of excuses and returned to my home office. Not that I needed a reason to do so. As the head of the company, I could pretty much do whatever I damn well pleased. But I had a strong work ethic, one that demanded one hundred ten percent on a daily basis. I hadn't gotten where I was by slacking off. And I intended to dismantle and absorb Harmony Developments in record time before moving on to the more pressing matter of ruining my father.

I sank into the chair behind my desk and groaned. A hangover clouded my brain, making coherent thought impossible. Otherwise, I would have been able to erase my ex-wife from it. The sight of her spread over my desk at Harmony Developments kept scrolling through my mind. I had to get a grip on my attraction to her before I did something stupid, like fuck her.

A light tap on my office door jerked me out of my head and back to business. Dahlia entered, looking collected and sexy, the way she always did. She gave me a warm smile, too warm in my opinion, and slid into the chair across from me. I watched her cross her legs with seductive slowness, a predatory gleam in her eyes. We were so over, and she just didn't seem to get it, even though I'd been nothing but upfront about my disinterest. Her obvious ploys were almost comical.

"I've got the resumes and applications for everyone at Harmony," she said. "I took the liberty of pulling all the ones I thought might interest you. The rejects are in this stack." She rested a perfectly manicured hand on the tallest stack of folders at the corner of my desk. The name on the top folder caught my eye. It was Dakota's.

"What's wrong with this one?" I asked, feeling an uncomfortable flutter at the sight of her name. Dakota Elaine Atwell. "She's got a contract."

"I just assumed you wouldn't be interested," Dahlia said, her voice smooth and cajoling. "You've got a dozen employees who can do her job. Why bother with the time and expense of training her for Infinity? She's redundant."

I slid the folder from beneath Dahlia's hand and flipped through the documents inside, although I'd already seen them. My sense of self-preservation told me to run as far and as fast from Dakota as possible. I'd loved her once. I hated her now, but I'd given Ansel my word. He seemed to hold quite an affection for her. She'd been the only sticking point in our negotiation. As much as I disliked her, she wasn't worth losing the company over. I could endure six months with her. I fully intended to stick her in a back office doing menial entry-level work then dump her. It would serve her right.

The rest of the day, she cluttered my thoughts, haunted

my meetings, and wreaked havoc on my focus. I could smell her perfume, taste the sweetness of her skin on my tongue, and feel the tight, wet heat of her wrapped around my cock. Thoughts like that had kept me semi-hard since lunch.

13

____

DAKOTA - NOW

I ARRIVED at the office early on Thursday, eager to catch up on emails and the tasks I'd missed the day before. Per the doctor's orders, I'd lounged on the sofa for the remainder of the previous day, injured foot propped in the air. It felt much better, and in spite of the assault to my fashion sensibilities, I wore a pair of nude flats with my favorite taupe skirt and a ruffled cream blouse. With my hair sleeked into a tight bun at the nape of my neck and a pair of black-rimmed glasses, I looked smart and aloof, sexy yet professional. Or at least that was the vibe I was going for.

By the light shining through the window of Sam's office, he'd beat me to work. I scrolled through my inbox with one eye on his door, praying he wouldn't come out. He didn't until well after ten o'clock, and when he did, he completely ignored me. Butterflies fluttered every time he walked past. I wasn't sure if I should be relieved or insulted by the snub, so I settled on apathetic. What did I care whether he talked to me or not? The less time we spent together, the less opportunity for him to slice me open with venomous barbs about my character.

My interoffice messenger pinged with an incoming message from Muriel.

Muriel: Did you check out the boss today?
Call the fire department.

Me: Why? Is he pissed again?

Muriel: He's smoking hot.

Me: I hadn't noticed.

Muriel: Are you blind?

Me: No, but I'm immune to tools and
douche nozzles.

I snickered at my cleverness and took a sip of coffee.

"I need you in my office, Ms. Atwell." The sound of Sam's voice behind me sent me into a panic. I jiggled the coffee cup, splashing hot liquid over the edges, making a mess of my workspace while simultaneously trying to close the messenger box.

"Shit," I muttered and grabbed a handful of tissues to dab away the spill.

Samuel stared down at me with cold, disapproving eyes. "You need one of those coffee cups with a spill-proof lid," he observed. "Or else you should wear something other than white." He turned to his office and spoke over his shoulder. "Grab your notes on MacGruder and come into the conference room."

I frowned down at the tan spots on my formerly pristine blouse.

"Now, Ms. Atwell."

What had happened to the patient boy of my past? This man radiated tension in every line of his body, from the square set of his shoulders down to the snap of his stride as he walked away. My insides quivered with dread as I gathered my information and followed him. I took a seat in the chair across from him, the table safely between us, and waited for him to speak first.

He went to the wall of windows and stared out at the city, his back to me. With his hands in his pockets, the fabric of his trousers stretched over his ass. It was hard and taut with indentations of muscle on each side. I swallowed and crossed my legs, squeezing my thighs together to fight the ache of lust between them.

During my reprieve yesterday, I'd decided that no reaction was the best course following our little sexual meltdown. Let him be the first one to broach the subject. Depending upon his attitude, I could then choose my best response. If he was angry, I would be cool. If he was insulting, I would be sweet. If he was…

"I think we should fuck it out," he said.

All of my potential retorts flew straight out of my head. Caught completely by surprise, I barked out a laugh. He didn't turn around, and I was grateful for a few seconds to pull myself together.

"I'm sorry. What did you say?" I asked when my voice returned. It shook a little, but I don't think he noticed.

"You heard me."

"Yes, I did, but it's the last thing I expected you to say." My heart resumed its chaotic dance inside my chest. At this rate, I might suffer a coronary before the end of the week. "I thought I wasn't worth it."

Mid-morning sunshine highlighted the angles of his face as he turned around. Muriel was right. In his impeccable suit, starched shirt, and red necktie, he made quite the picture. His features remained smooth. When our eyes met, I saw nothing but green ice in them.

"You're not," he replied in a tone so matter-of-fact, the remnants of my self-worth quivered. "But for whatever reason, I'm still attracted to you. And I hate myself for it."

Because I didn't know what to say, I said nothing. We stared at each other across the room.

He exhaled through his nose as if disappointed in his fate. "One last time. Sort of a going-away fuck, if you will."

It took a few seconds for his statement to sink in and when it did, it dropped like a brick to the pit of my gut. "That's hardly the kind of invitation a girl wants to hear." I inhaled through my nose, steadying myself.

"Too harsh for you?" he asked. "Or too honest?"

"I don't sleep with my coworkers." On the outside I probably appeared reserved, but inside I was doing a happy dance. He still wanted me. In a game where he held all the cards, this tidbit of knowledge gave me the teeniest bit of power. A thrill of female triumph lessened the anxiety of the previous days. For the smallest second, I considered accepting his offer, eager to revisit the strength of his body moving over and inside me, the stretch of his muscular thighs between mine, and the glide of his bare chest against my breasts. My stomach twittered. Tangled up in my lust were the remnants of our emotional intimacy as man and wife. Instinctively, I knew I couldn't have one without interference by the other. Common sense took hold as I watched him. This was a competition. One I intended to win. A hasty decision made today might result in defeat tomorrow.

"Is that so?" His eyes gleamed with a shrewd intensity that unnerved me. I shook my head. "Never?"

"Never." I extended my index finger into the air to detail my objections. "First, it's unprofessional as well as unethical." He nodded, considering. I swallowed and continued. "Second, by your own admission, you hate me. And third, you've been nothing but shitty to me all week. Why would I want to have sex with you?"

He stroked his scruffy jaw thoughtfully. I followed the movement of his fingers as they moved up and down, mesmerized by the slow, sensual motion and the memory of his fingers doing that very same thing to me. A glimmer of humor lit his eyes. He shrugged. "Fair enough. I just thought I would throw it out there as an option—to relieve the tension."

Ignoring his scrutiny, I opened the MacGruder folder and spread my notes over the table in front of me. If I had any chance at all of salvaging my career, I needed to keep our relationship professional. "So what do you want to know about MacGruder?"

My first job out of college was working for MacGruder & Sons, the premier real estate broker of the Midwest. They were famous for snatching up obscure parcels of land and selling them for exorbitant prices to developers. The senior MacGruder, John, had an eye for potential growth areas and an almost psychic ability for knowing trends in real estate. If there was a new shopping mall or suburb in the works, chances were good MacGruder & Sons had their hands in it. The sons, on the other hand, were more of a liability than an asset to the company.

Samuel moved easily from the topic of revenge-fucks back to business. He unbuttoned his suit jacket, removed it, and hung it over the back of a chair. I expected him to sit across the table, but instead, he took the seat next to me. The scent of his cologne drifted past me, breaking my concentration. I remembered that smell, spicy and rich. The man might have changed, but his cologne hadn't. His shirt-sleeve brushed my forearm, and all the tiny hairs from wrist to elbow stood at attention.

"I want to know everything. Where they hang out. What they eat for breakfast." He leaned across me to touch my notes with one big hand.

"That's a little creepy," I said lightly. "May I ask why?"

"No. You may not." The flat finality in his voice should have quaffed my interest, but it served to do the opposite. I studied him, taking in the square line of his jaw and the sharp straight line of his nose.

"What you really want to know are their flaws," I said. "Their weaknesses."

"Yes." When he shifted to face me, I shifted with him, mirroring his movement from force of a habit I'd thought long forgotten. "Tell me something I can use to make this happen, Dakota."

For the first time since our acquaintance, he said my name without anger or resentment. The way his baritone slid over the vowels and enunciated the consonants sent a tingle straight between my legs. Encouraged by his interest and heartened by a subject I knew well, I complied with enthusiasm. I stood and leaned over him to move a pile of folders across the table, letting my breasts graze his shoulder, taking advantage of his attraction to goad him a bit.

"Well, as you know, there's the old man, John, and his two sons, Jared and Junior. John's sharp. He knows the market. He follows the trends. He sees potential where others see nothing." I tapped a finger on an article I'd printed from the pages of the *Wall Street Journal.* "He knew about this shopping center outside of Chicago years before it became viable." It was now a multi-million-dollar property, spawning a bevy of strip malls and restaurants. Several housing developments had popped up nearby. "MacGruder bought all this land at rock-bottom prices from a farmer's widow then turned around and sold it at a hundred times his investment."

"I already know that," Samuel said with barely veiled impatience. "I need more than that to work with."

I frowned and scanned my notes, wracking my brain for any useful tidbit of information. After a second, I reached across the table for my laptop. Sam's eyes drifted to the sliver of cleavage revealed by the throat of my blouse. My nipples tightened in response. I cleared my throat and tried not to think about the dimple in his chin or the size of his hands resting on the table, the way one of them could cup my breast, the feel of his lips on the tender skin.

"There is this." I pulled up an article on my laptop and turned it to face Sam, showing him the headline. "MacGruder bought these two tracts of land on the outskirts of St. Louis. He way overpaid for the purchase. It was completely unlike him. Given the current market, he stands to lose his ass if he can't turn it around."

Sam leaned back, brow furrowed. By the spark of interest in his eyes, I'd hit on something of value.

"That's good. St. Louis, you say?" He rubbed his chin. "Get me all the information you can find on this."

"I've got it all right here." I pulled out a second file and handed it to him, grateful I'd had the foresight to print out copies of the articles.

"What about the sons? What can you tell me about them? You dated Jared. Surely you picked up something useful during that time." He kicked back in his chair and swiveled to face me directly. The weight of his curious gaze traveled over me.

He knew about Jared? I'd always assumed he'd erased me from his mind the minute I'd walked out his door with my suitcase in hand and divorce papers on the kitchen table. But he hadn't. He stared. I stared back then ducked my head to hide the guilty flush on my cheeks. I wasn't sure why I felt like I'd betrayed him by dating someone after our divorce. He certainly had moved on, and I had attempted to do the same. Maybe, it was my own heart that felt betrayed, because I denied it of the one person it loved.

"It wasn't like that," I said, returning my gaze to his, feeling the need to excuse my actions. "We went to a few business dinners after I left the company to come here. Nothing more." I squared my shoulders and lifted my chin. "I told you—I don't date my coworkers."

"Right." His one-word acknowledgment showed he clearly didn't believe me, and why should he? In his opinion, I was the kind of girl who valued money over love and ethics.

A kernel of tension blossomed between my brows. Efforts to change his opinion of me were futile, so I returned my focus to his original question. "Jared's a hothead. He spends money on frivolous things—money, women, cars, underground fights. Junior's a bit dull. No head for business. And the two brothers butt heads constantly."

I stretched across the table to grab a second report. The throat of my blouse fell open. Sam's gaze drifted to my cleavage again. A spark of lust flickered in his eyes. When his focus returned to my face, a flush spread up his neck and into his cheeks. I tried not to smirk, reveling in his embarrassment.

"They butted heads over you." His words sounded more like an accusation than a statement.

The walls of my throat constricted. How could he possibly know? No one knew except the parties concerned; at least, that was what I'd thought. Had he been watching me over the years? The chair I was sitting in became uncomfortably hard. I shifted and tried to put the idea out of my mind.

His cellphone rang. He glanced down at the display then lifted the phone to his ear. "Hey, babe." The simple endearment prickled my skin with a hot wave of jealousy. He'd talked to me that way once upon a time. A sudden pang of longing bowled me over, to be the girl on the other side of the conversation, to be his. "Yeah. Tonight's good." He cupped a hand over the phone. "You can go now, Dakota." I started to gather the documents into the folder. He stopped me with a touch of his hand on mine. "Leave it."

I nodded, irritated with myself for caring, for remembering, for being jealous. I leaned over and said, loud enough for the other person to hear, "Anything you say, baby."

He frowned. His gaze locked with mine and didn't let me go as he said to the person on the other end of the line, "I expect you in my bed naked when I get there."

A thousand shards of glass sliced into my heart. We'd been divorced for a decade. We were strangers to each other, but the idea of him in bed with someone else wounded me like we'd only broken up yesterday. Not to mention the way he'd propositioned me only an hour earlier and so easily slid into the arms of another woman. Was Brian right? Had my Sam become a manwhore?

I felt sick as I left the room and took up residence in my

cubicle once more. I stared at the computer screen, unseeing. The man in the office behind me was no one I'd ever known. I just couldn't wrap my mind around the man he'd grown into. I missed the old Sam, the one whose green eyes had shown with appreciation every time he saw me, whose laughter had warmed my skin, and whose smiles had chased away the gray on the rainiest of days. Suddenly, I wanted nothing more than to see that boy one more time, to tell him how much he meant to me, and beg him to never change.

14

SAMUEL - NOW

WITH A groan, I passed a hand over my face. I'd promised to meet Tuck and Beckett for a game of basketball after work, something I usually looked forward to. Not today. Today I wanted to hide in the corner of some dark bar with a bottle of bourbon and try to drink away the vision of my ex-wife's face. Oh, wait. I'd tried that and had the vestiges of a hangover to prove it.

They were already on the court when I arrived at the gym. Beckett, sly bastard, took one look at my face and smirked. "You look like shit. Ever think about shaving?" Always clean-cut, Becks loved to give me a hard time over my aversion to the razor.

I scratched a finger over the stubble on my chin. "Not today," I admitted. "I've had other things on my mind."

"When you're that pretty, you don't have to shave." Tuck tossed the basketball at me. I caught it, but my limbs felt heavy and thick. I shot it back at him and tripped over the boundary line.

"What's your excuse then?" I asked him. Tuck had the

carefully messy look that drove women wild. His blond hair was longer and darker than mine, pulled into a ponytail. A neatly trimmed beard outlined his jaw. I'd never seen him in anything dressier than jeans and a T-shirt, but then, he spent most of his time in front of a computer monitor, designing video games.

"There is no excuse for Tuck." Beckett lunged forward, stole the ball from Tuck's hands, and drove for the basket. We both stood in place and watched him dunk the ball.

"Show-off," I grumbled. A former college basketball star, Beckett excelled at everything he did. He landed lightly on the balls of his feet and shot us a grin.

"So how's life in the corporate world?" Tucker asked. "You done with that merger yet?"

"Not yet." I caught Beckett's pass and dribbled the ball from hand to hand, avoiding both men's gazes, unprepared for their inevitable ribbing. "I've run into a complication."

"Don't tell me you're getting soft in your old age," Beckett interjected. He faked an attempt to grab the ball. I blocked him with an outstretched arm. It was a token effort. He was by far the better athlete among the three of us and could have annihilated my defense without breaking a sweat. "You said you'd be in and out in a week."

"My ex-wife works there." I dodged Beckett's hand for a second time and made an awkward drive for the basket. Neither guy came after me. When I turned, they were standing there, gaping like I knew they'd be.

"You're divorced? Christ, I didn't even know you'd been married." This came from Beckett. He ran a hand through his short, dark hair. Tucker rubbed the back of his neck. He knew about Dakota and the divorce, having experienced the aftermath firsthand as my college roommate. I didn't meet Beckett until after graduation, when Dakota was long gone from my life. I sent the ball to Tuck with a chest pass. He caught it and secured it under an arm, bringing the game to a halt.

"What?" I bent down to evade their gazes and retied my shoelace, even though it was perfectly tight.

"Holy shit, man. You've been sitting on this information all week and didn't think to share?" Tuck exchanged a look with Becks.

"It's no big deal," I said. "Just a nuisance."

"Are you okay?" Tucker asked, a teasing grin on his tanned face. "Do you want to talk about your feelings and shit? Cause we're totally here for you, bro, if that's what you need."

I groaned and shook my head. "This is precisely why I didn't say anything. It was a long time ago." I dragged a forearm across my forehead, feeling the effects of last night's bourbon. Sweat poured out of me, soaking my shirt, even though we'd been on the court for less than twenty minutes.

Beckett broke his silence. "Is that why you've been acting so weird this week?" His brows lowered. He shot a glance at Tucker. "I called him today, and in the middle of the conversation he told me to be naked and on his bed when he got home. Then he says he was playing a joke on someone and to disregard. I'm starting to worry."

Tucker chuckled, mirthful and mischievous as a seventh grader. "Has she turned you off women? 'Cause I've totally heard of that happening before."

Shit. I'd totally forgotten about Beckett's call during our meeting this morning. Eager for retribution, I'd invented that little tidbit just to see the reaction on her face, and it had been priceless. "Sorry about that," I said to Beckett and shot Tucker a glare. "I'm still into women, thank you. You're too hairy for my taste, Beckett." I swiped a hand over my face and searched for the words to describe the situation. I didn't want any kind of emotional involvement with Dakota. She was about as trustworthy as rattlesnake. Unfortunately, my dick hadn't received the message and was still perking up at the mere thought of her.

"So this woman? She's the reason you're such a heartbreaker. Am I right?" The pieces of the puzzle snapped into place for Beckett as he studied my face. "Unable to commit. Serial one-night stands. Aversion to dating."

"Yeah. I guess," I said. We'd given up the pretense of playing ball by this time. Beckett and Tucker, in true form, found my predicament much more interesting than a mundane game of basketball. In unspoken agreement, we grabbed our gear from the sidelines and headed toward the showers.

"Have you actually talked to her?" Beckett asked.

"It's hard not to," I replied, feeling a small amount of relief to discuss the problem with someone. "She's actually pretty good at what she does, and I need her to make my next project work."

"But you're going to can her." Tucker tossed the basketball into the equipment cage, voice full of confidence. He turned his attention to Beckett. "This girl really did a number on him. Sold out to his dad for a big fat check." Beckett looked appropriately shocked. "So he's going to throw her out on her ass. Isn't that right, Seaforth?" Tucker locked his gaze onto me.

I shifted uncomfortably from foot to foot. "That was the plan, but she's got a contract," I said. "I'm stuck with her for a while." No need to go into the whole fatal-attraction situation. As far as they knew, I'd never cared for a woman beyond what she might do for me in bed or in the boardroom, and I planned to keep it that way. "Unless I can get her to quit. And believe me, I'm having a great time trying."

Beckett laughed. "No wonder you look like hell. That's got to be a bitch. Facing your ex every day."

"Why don't you just buy her out?" Tucker asked. His gaze flicked away from mine and toward the girls entering the gym. "She's money-hungry, right? Just write her a check and say goodbye." The women drew closer. He flashed a devastating smile at the tall blonde with a huge rack. "Hey, ladies."

"Hi," she said, turning her focus from Tuck to me. "Hi, Sam."

"Hi, Cadence," I said, feeling an instant frisson of dread. I'd hooked up with this girl a few times, casual sex after random encounters at a nightclub hangout. She was centerfold gorgeous with legs longer than mine and a blinding smile. Our last rendezvous had been over a month ago.

"How've you been?"

"Good. How about you?" I stood there, feeling guilty but not sure why. We'd never gone on a date, never exchanged phone numbers, and never set any expectations beyond mutual gratification. I didn't even know her last name. In retrospect, it seemed cheap and shallow, a veiled attempt to satisfy my physical needs without emotional detachment. Before marrying Dakota, I hated guys like me. Reconnecting with her made me see who I'd become. I loathed what I saw.

"Fine. Busy," she said. The stilted awkwardness of our conversation lingered in the air between us. Even though we'd seen each other naked in a variety of embarrassing positions, our discomfort was palpable. She gestured to the quiet girl standing beside her. "This is my friend, Lauren.

Lauren, this is Sam." Cadence blinked her gaze to Tuck, eyes bright with interest. He said I was the one who got all the girls, but in truth, it was him.

I hesitated, words forming a knot in my throat. The need to excuse my bad behavior welled up inside my head. I had no idea how to begin an apology of this kind.

"Don't mind him. He's got no manners. I'm Tuck, and this is Beckett." Tuck extended his hand to Cadence. They exchanged a long look between each other. In that moment, I knew I'd lost another one to him but didn't care. I'd fucked this gorgeous girl six ways from Sunday, but all I could think about was how Dakota's hair was longer, her lips fuller, and eyes prettier than this girl's. Fuck. I scraped a hand over my face, trying to remove the images and failing miserably. The reality of the situation glared at me. Even when Dakota was gone, I still carried her with me. I guess I always had.

15

DAKOTA - NOW

ON FRIDAY, I wore a gray jersey knit dress that hugged all my best features and skimmed over the less desirable ones. While the dress had a conservative neckline, the clingy fabric made my breasts look higher and fuller than they actually were. Beneath the dress, I wore a silky pair of thigh-high stockings, sans panties. The silk rubbed against the sensitive skin of my inner thighs every time I took a step. I felt decadent and naughty, and the sensation gave me new confidence.

When Sam called me into the conference room to go over our schedule for the day, I sat down next to him and made sure he got a peek at the elastic of the stockings through the slit in the skirt. His Adam's apple bobbed when I uncrossed and crossed my legs for a third then fourth time. I pretended not to notice, but it gave me a modicum of satisfaction, especially when he asked me to pick up his tuxedo from the dry cleaners on the opposite side of the city in under thirty minutes.

"You're kidding me," I said. "There's no way I can make

it over there and back in less than hour." I swore he did things like that just to test my limits.

"I didn't ask for your opinion on the matter." His eyes gleamed with challenge, one I readily accepted. As uncomfortable as our relationship might be, I was beginning to enjoy the rub between us.

"In case you weren't aware, I'm not your personal assistant," I said in a pleasant, conversational tone. "Maybe you should ask Valerie or Sadie to run your errands for you. Or here's an idea," I added brightly. "Maybe you could hire someone to babysit you."

"Are you refusing an assignment, Ms. Atwell?" he asked. One corner of his mouth curled up in sadistic amusement. "Because that could be considered insubordination. And I do believe your contract has a clause allowing for your dismissal without remuneration in such a case."

We stared at each other. His eyes met mine, relentless and smoldering. Heat crept through my limbs, starting in my fingers and coursing all the way to my toes. I admired adversarial Sam, the way his jaw ticked with irritation and his nostrils flared like a cat scenting its prey. He was all alpha, all male, and sexy as hell.

"Why do you need a tuxedo in the middle of the day anyway? Do you have some kind of formal lunch or something?" I toyed with the chain around my neck, enjoying the way his focus lingered on my fingers. "Because it's not on the agenda for today."

"None of your business, Ms. Atwell." He blinked up to my lips then to my eyes. The intensity of his gaze made my pulse flutter. For the briefest second, I wondered how it would feel to be kissed again by those lips, if he still tasted of mint, if his mouth was as soft as I remembered. A dull ache of need throbbed between my legs. I uncrossed my legs again and stood.

"Are you going to need anything else?" I asked when he was finished.

"No," he said absently, and then shook his head. "I mean, yes. Where is the report on Stone Creek Properties? I'm going to need it for Monday."

I bit my lower lip, thinking. "I put it in your bottom file drawer."

"I looked there and didn't see it," he said, clearly distracted. He rubbed a finger over his upper lip.

"I'm pretty sure it's there." I crossed the room to his desk and bent over to open the drawer, giving him a full view of my backside. When I drew closer to him, file in hand, his eyes had grown dark.

He ran a hand around the inside of his collar, as if loosening a constriction.

"See? Here it is." I placed the file in his upturned palm and brushed past him on my way to the door.

He didn't come out of the office for the rest of the morning.

Muriel stared at me with a frown as I scanned the daily menu. We were waiting in line to order our food at the cafeteria downstairs, the first time I'd eaten lunch all week. I stared at the list of items, unable to find anything appetizing. I liked to eat—a lot and often—but this business with Samuel had my stomach tied up in knots.

"What are you doing?" Muriel nudged my shoulder impatiently. The red-and-yellow plastic bracelets around her wrist clinked against each other with the motion. She looked tropical and exotic in a dress adorned with colorful tulips.

"Oh, sorry." I glanced over my shoulder at the people crowding behind us and moved forward.

"No. I mean what's up with you and the hunk?" Muriel's canny brown eyes narrowed. "He watches you like you're about to steal the family silver or something. The tension between you two is off the charts."

I choked on a sip of iced tea. She thumped me on my back until I gasped, unaware of the accuracy of her statement. Inside my purse, my cellphone buzzed with an incoming call. I ignored it and turned my gaze back to the food.

"Nothing is up with me and Mr. Seaforth," I said, my tongue stumbling over the formal address. "Except he hates me."

The server plopped a roll onto my tray. We fell silent as we moved to the next station.

"Did something happen between you two?" She lowered her voice and leaned toward me. "I mean, he took your office away and gave it to the bitch-troll." A shiver shook her thin shoulders. "And he moved you to a cubicle. Why would he do that?"

I bit my lower lip to keep from pouring out the entire story for two reasons. One, none of my coworkers knew I'd been married, however briefly. I preferred to avoid the inevitable questions regarding the breakup. And two, I didn't want anyone to think I received preferential treatment of any kind from the boss. I knew how these things worked. Rumors sparked and caught fire in the corporate environment like a match to a haystack. No matter how untrue, that kind of gossip could wreck my career.

"I don't know." I shrugged and summoned a smile, afraid I'd said too much.

"Rumor has it he's going to dismantle Harmony Enterprises," Muriel said in a hushed whisper. "They say he's going to close the doors and take a select few back to his corporate office."

I stared at her, disbelieving. The knots in my stomach tightened. "We're a viable business. He wouldn't do that." I spoke with confidence, but deep down I wondered. Would he? I didn't know him. Not really. Not anymore.

"They say he's got his eye on a new business and that Harmony Enterprises is just a stepping stone to cornering the market." Her bracelets clanked against each other as she added sugar to her iced tea and stirred.

We fell silent and carried our trays to an empty table. It was a beautiful spring day. The rain from earlier in the week had cleared, and bright sunshine streamed in the giant windows beside our table. My phone buzzed again. I reached to check the caller ID and frowned at the unfamiliar number.

"Hello?" I asked.

"Where are you? I need you in my office. Now." Sam's voice, low and commanding, sent a prickle of gooseflesh across my back. I'd forgotten how smooth and masculine his voice was, the way it affected me, shimmering over my ear.

"Who is this?" I knew damn good and well who it was but couldn't resist yanking his chain.

"You know who it is," he responded, an undercurrent of irritation in his tone. "Why aren't you at your desk?"

"It's lunch time. I'll be up as soon as I'm finished." I ended the call, feeling the knot of dread in my stomach loosen the smallest bit.

"Was that him?" Muriel asked, eyes widening in disbelief. "You talk to him that way?"

"He's infuriating. He basically said he plans to make my life hell for the next six months or until I quit." I took a bite of my sandwich and forced it down.

"He said that?" She dropped her sandwich back to her plate. "He really doesn't like you."

"That might be the understatement of the year," I replied. The second bite of sandwich tasted better than the first. Plain ham and cheese on wheat. A dill pickle. Sam's favorites. He was everywhere, in my dreams, my workplace, and my lunch. It seemed he was unavoidable.

"Or maybe he has the hots for you." She leaned forward conspiratorially and raised a thin, penciled eyebrow. "Maybe he wants to sex you up, and it pisses him off."

I stared at her, amazed by her intuition. I thought about his hands pushing up the hem of my skirt as he'd lain me on his desk. The way his lips ignited my skin. The tortured look on his face when he'd dismissed me, and his proposition. *Maybe we should fuck it out.*

"Uh-oh. Incoming." Muriel's voice interrupted my epiphany.

"What?" A prickle of awareness crawled up my spine. I knew without looking that Samuel was standing behind me. The cafeteria had grown quiet. Curious gazes turned in my direction.

"Atwell. Upstairs. Now."

The menacing tone spurred my rebellious nature. It must be something pretty important if he'd come all the way downstairs, thirty-seven floors, to collect me. Not one of his minions, nor the bitch-troll Dahlia. Samuel himself.

"In a minute. I'm still eating." My gaze met Muriel's.

One corner of her mouth curled in a repressed grin. I took another bite of my sandwich.

"This can't wait." He moved to stand in front of me, blocking my view with six-plus feet of male pulchritude. His ominous shadow fell across the table.

I raised an eyebrow and looked up into his face. "Don't you know it's rude to interrupt someone when they're eating?" I asked. "Besides, I get a thirty-minute lunch."

"You're salaried," he replied, his voice quiet but still intimidating. "You don't get shit."

"Fire me." I took another bite of my sandwich, relishing the taste all the more because of his irritation.

"God, I would love that." A small glimmer of amusement sparked deep within the emerald depths of his gaze. "But I can't. So quit playing around. I need you upstairs. Hell, bring your sandwich, if you're that attached to it."

With a melodramatic sigh, I conceded, wrapped my sandwich in a napkin, and shoved it into my purse, knowing I'd never get to eat it. "Fine. What's the fire?"

"I've got a meeting with MacGruder this afternoon, and I want you to go with me."

16

DAKOTA - NOW

THE SAME silver BMW I'd seen outside the coffee shop met us at the curb in front of our building twenty minutes later. The driver, dressed in a smart black suit, opened the door for me. I glanced up into the face of Rockwell, now silver-haired with lines creasing his mild features. He smiled back at me and winked.

"Good afternoon, Ms. Atwell," he said. "It's a pleasure to see you again."

"You too, Rockwell," I replied with genuine warmth.

My mind should have been on the upcoming meeting and I was curious about its purpose, but my thoughts kept straying to all the times I'd been in the car with Samuel before our divorce. The first time we'd made love in his Porsche at the park. The ratty Subaru we'd driven for the duration of our marriage. The way his hand used to steal across the console to rest on my thigh. My gaze rested on his hand, palm down atop his thigh, forefinger tapping a merciless rhythm. A glance at his features suggested nothing more than controlled calm, but I recognized the gesture. He was nervous about something. I squelched the instinct to take his hand in mine, to soothe his worry, and curled my fingers into my palm.

A hunger pang twisted my stomach. It growled, breaking the silence in the car.

He shot me an exasperated look. "Can't you do something about that? It sounds like you've got an alien in there."

"Don't start with me," I warned. "It's your fault."

He scrubbed a hand over his face, but I had the feeling he was hiding a laugh. I glared at him, daring him to say something more. He ducked his head and coughed. Feeling smug for no reason, I settled deeper into the seat. It was very comfortable.

"So are you going to tell me why I'm here?" I asked. "I can't help you if I don't know my purpose. I don't want to say the wrong thing."

Several minutes passed before Samuel answered. I flinched at the sound of his voice, having given up on his response and turned my attention to the streetscape outside the car.

"I want to buy MacGruder," he said, his voice gravelly and hushed. "They need to sell. They just don't know it yet."

I laughed at the absurdity of his idea. Samuel glowered. "Are you crazy? He'll never sell. His father started that company and he wants his sons to take over."

Samuel turned to regard me, his gaze predatorily bright. "You said yourself his sons are uninterested. That they're incapable of running the business."

"You know it and I know it, but MacGruder will never admit it." I nudged his knee with mine to emphasize my point and immediately regretted it. For a split second, I'd forgotten we were adversaries and had fallen into the intimacy of our old relationship. His focus dipped to the contact, a small frown drooping the corners of his mouth, and I shifted away from him. "You know how fathers are. They dream of passing their empires on to their sons." *Like your father,* I added silently.

"That's where you come in. We need to show him the error of his ways," he said.

"We?"

"He likes you. Trusts you. I want him to feel the trust."

The car stopped. I glanced up to find us parked in front of my apartment building. "Wait. What are we doing here?"

"You can't go to a meeting dressed like that." Sam's gaze flickered over my outfit and, as always, tan spots of coffee dotted the front of my dress. He raised an eyebrow. "Something a little more—" He waved a hand across his chest in a helpless male gesture. I sighed and rolled my eyes. "Make it dazzling."

I jumped out of the car before Rockwell could open the door for me, overwhelmed by irritation and embarrassment. Dazzling? Seriously? I sprinted off the elevator and into my apartment, shedding my clothes on the way to my bedroom closet. After a furious inventory of my wardrobe, I settled on a fitted black dress with cap sleeves and a peplum ruffle at the waist. It emphasized my narrow waist, giving me an hourglass figure. Black pumps combined with the mid-thigh length of the hem, gave the illusion of long legs. After a quick touch of lip gloss and mascara, I twisted my hair into a messy, sexy updo. Still professional but enticing and, combined with my schoolteacher spectacles, a sassy mix.

I'd just stepped into the elevator when a text came across my phone. Samuel. *Today, Atwell,* was all it said. I'd been less than ten minutes. Irritation brought a low growl from my throat and a look of cautious concern from the mother holding the hand of a small boy beside me.

Bite me, I texted and pressed send before I could rethink it.

Samuel stood on the sidewalk, phone to his ear when I exited the building. A light breeze ruffled his hair. My consternation dissipated a bit when I saw surprise then heated appreciation flash through his eyes as he turned to face me. He stopped talking mid-sentence and drew his gaze over me. His nostrils flared and his eyes darkened in a male gesture that sent an electric tingle throughout my insides. Score one for Dakota. Rockwell stepped forward. Samuel waved him away, opened the car door for me, and resumed his phone conversation.

We drove to the other side of the city. He continued his conversation in French, eyes firmly fixed on my legs. My French was rusty, but I caught the words "merger," "hostile," and "death" somewhere in there. For the hundredth time that day, I marveled at the strangeness of the man beside me. He spoke quickly and easily, running a hand through his hair, with none of the easygoing manner of my ex-husband. I slowly uncrossed and crossed my legs, pausing to rub my calves together, soothing an imaginary itch. He swallowed, and his conversation stumbled.

A glimmer of an idea began to form in my head. I smirked, eager to take advantage of our close proximity. As long as he intended to torture me with petty errands and meaningless tasks, I intended to toy with his attraction to me.

"What?" Samuel asked, his voice deeper and raspier than before. He'd ended his call but kept the phone in his grasp.

"Better?" I leveled my eyes with his, challenging him.

"Better," he said on an exhale, once again dragging his gaze along my body.

His cellphone buzzed. He pulled his attention from me and scrolled through the text messages, but not before I caught a glimpse of the name of the caller: Dahlia. A flash of the slim, well-dressed blonde filled my memory, the way she touched his arm, proprietary and knowing, at the meeting on Monday. Jealousy prickled through my veins. I swallowed it back and shook my head at the absurdity of the emotion. He wasn't mine. I willingly gave up any claims to him years ago, so why did the idea of him with someone else bother me so freaking much?

"Your girlfriend?" I asked. "Obviously, you don't worry about sexual harassment suits from your employees."

"I don't do girlfriends." Samuel tapped out a return text then tucked the phone back into his pocket. "I have sex with other consenting adults."

"Like the one on the phone this morning?" I let the hem of my dress ride up my thighs, enjoying the way his gaze kept traveling back to my legs and the red patches high on his cheeks when I caught him in the act.

"Yes. And others." He swallowed hard when I trailed a finger over my collarbone. "Believe it or not, there are plenty of women eager to sleep with me, and I take full advantage of the opportunity."

To cover my jealousy, I fiddled with the gold chain around my neck, careful to keep the end of it tucked inside my dress. His eyes held mine. I swallowed hard and tried to keep a cool head. "But there's not any special one?"

"No." His gaze flicked to my chest for a fraction of a second and my traitorous nipples tightened, showing plainly through the clingy knit. I'd never seen such heat in a man's eyes before. "What about you? Do you date, Dakota, or do you fuck?"

I chose not to answer, but let a secretive smile curve my lips instead. His expression darkened. There was no one in my life, but he didn't need to know that. The fingers of his left hand tapped out an unconscious rhythm on top of his thigh. I kept my gaze locked with his.

"No special man in your life? I can't believe you don't have someone warming your bed at night." He cocked his head to one side and lifted an eyebrow. "Or maybe a rich old man ready to kick the bucket?"

"Do you think about my bed, Sam? It's quite warm, I assure you." We stared at each other, mutual lust and animosity heating the space between us. "But for your information, I don't do relationships either."

"So you just fuck then?" The deep rasp of his voice raked over me, sending a heated chill down my back.

"Sometimes." The air felt hot and thick inside the car. "Sometimes I screw." His mouth parted, and he ran the tip of his tongue over his lower lip. "And sometimes I take care of myself." As I spoke, I trailed a hand up and down my thigh, letting the hem of my dress ride higher. He drew his lip between his teeth. He'd never been able to resist when I touched myself in front of him. Some things never changed, I guessed. My heart beat a little faster knowing I could still turn him on with just words.

"Like where?" By this time, he'd dropped the phone into his pocket and both hands curled into fists on top of his legs until the knuckles turned white.

"In the shower." I twitched my thighs together, soothing a pretend itch, teasing him. "On the sofa." His throat convulsed as he swallowed. The front of his pants stretched over his growing bulge. Recognizing the signs of imminent triumph, I went in for the kill. "At my desk."

"Jesus," he muttered.

The car swerved as tires squealed beside us. My purse tumbled onto the floor, spilling its contents. Sam threw out an arm to steady me and glared at Rockwell, breaking the fragile magical thread binding us moments earlier.

"Sorry, sir," Rockwell said. "Some idiot ran a red light."

I'd forgotten about him. Had he been listening to our conversation? How could he not? Mortified, I lifted my gaze to meet his in the rearview mirror. His smile was polite but nothing more.

Sam laughed, a full-bellied guffaw, at my look of utter horror. "I wish you could see your face right now."

"Shut up," I hissed. The temperature inside the car had risen about ten degrees higher, all of it centering in my cheeks. "You're an ass."

He smiled, showing more dimples than should be legal. I wrinkled my nose and scowled before bending to retrieve my belongings from the floor. Lipstick, breath mints, birth control pills, tampons.

"I don't know how you think I can help you today," I said, eager to change the subject and shift his attention away from the tampon in my hand. I stuffed it into my purse.

"If you want to keep your job, you'll figure something out," he said.

"I'm starting to think it isn't worth it," I grumbled.

His answering snort of satisfaction caused my mouth to snap shut. I tugged at the hem of my dress and shifted toward the window. Billowy white clouds rolled through an azure sky. The buildings became newer and taller. Samuel leaned forward, tapped Rockwell on the shoulder, and murmured something in his ear. Classical music, soft and soothing, poured through the sound system and filled the uncomfortable silence.

A few minutes later, the car stopped in front of the Seaforth Towers. The contents of my hastily eaten sandwich churned in my stomach. I hadn't been this close to Maxwell Seaforth in ten years. Just knowing he was near brought back a flood of unpleasant memories. I cast a curious glance at Sam, wondering how he felt about visiting his father's building. When I'd last known them, their relationship had been fraught with conflict, mainly over me. Judging by the car, Rockwell, and Sam's financial status, father and son had managed to repair the rift between them. It gave me more satisfaction than I realized, to see Sam living the lifestyle he'd been born into, and to know my absence from his life had been beneficial.

The twin buildings stretched up, up, and up into the sky. I craned my neck to see the top of them. They were an architectural testament to Seaforth's success, monuments to his ego. The location was also a marker of MacGruder's advancement into the big leagues. When I'd worked for them, they resided in a nineteenth century limestone building in Old Towne with intermittent air conditioning and hot water. This building was newly constructed, unconventional, and very impressive. Rockwell came around to open the door. He extended a gloved hand to help me out. I took it, my smile returning at the sight of a friendly face.

"You look lovely," he said, blue eyes crinkling at the corners. "Your mother must be very proud of you."

I cringed but found no sarcasm in his expression, nothing but sincerity and warmth. "Thanks, Rockwell," I said, blushing a little at the compliment. "You look great, too." I tried to calm my racing pulse. "You didn't happen to hear any of our conversation, did you?" My eyebrows lifted and my gaze darted to Sam then back to Rockwell.

"No. I was wearing my earbuds." He gestured to the wire hanging around his neck, inside the collar of his shirt. "I wanted to give you some privacy. Why?" Rockwell's brow furrowed.

"Um, no reason." I gave him a sunny smile, relief washing over me.

"If you two are done kissing each other's ass?" Samuel shrugged into his suit coat, buttoning up the jacket, tugging down the cuffs with tanned fingers. Diamond cufflinks winked in the bright sunlight.

"Who is this guy?" I asked Rockwell, rolling my eyes. "What happened to him?"

"You did, Miss," he replied, his expression sobering.

17

SAMUEL - THEN

EACH TUESDAY, my mother held a formal dinner for a few of her intimate friends and business colleagues of my father. I hated those dinners more than a trip to the dentist. The older I became, the less tolerance I possessed for conversations about stock trends, the costliness of summer homes, and legal proceedings. In order to evade an evening of torture, I began to invent homework and after school events, anything to keep me from sitting at that twelve-foot table in a suit and tie with people twice my age.

"Are you sure you can't stay?" Mother asked for the third time in the space of ten minutes. She stood in front of her dressing table, sleeking back her hair with a graceful hand. "The Barretts are coming, and they're bringing Clover. I thought maybe you could entertain her."

I suppressed a groan. Clover Barrett was a vain redhead a few years younger than me who always talked in a high-pitched baby's voice about clothes and nail polish and how many boys asked her out over lunch break. "No. Sorry," I said. "Vanessa can hang out with her."

"You know your sister and Clover don't get along," Mother said. I watched her draw a tube of red lipstick over her mouth. Her gaze met mine in the reflection of the mirror. "Are you going to see that Atwell girl?"

"Her name's Dakota, Mom," I said. "Why don't you ever say her name?"

"It's a silly name, don't you think?" She stood and smoothed her hands over the silk of her brown dress.

"No sillier than Clover. Who names their kid after a cow?"

She laughed. The rare sound rewarded me with a flood of warmth. I wondered why she didn't smile more. Were her days so sad? From the outside, her life looked picture perfect with its circle of friends, social events, and frequent trips to tropical beaches. If she had troubles, she hid them well from me. I'd never seen her raise her voice to anyone or heard my parents argue, but then, my father wasn't around much.

"You spend a lot of time with that girl. Your father doesn't approve. He'll ground you again if you don't show tonight." I watched her move to the jewelry cabinet next to the closet and remove a strand of pearls. She draped it gracefully around her neck. "Help me with the clasp, would you?"

"He's been pretty vocal about it," I admitted as I locked the clasp at the nape of her neck. "You don't like her either."

"It's not that I don't like her. She's very intelligent, and her mother is a dear. I don't know what I'd do without her. What that woman can do with a pastry is amazing." She turned to face me and laid a palm against my cheek, her eyes soft and adoring. "I just think you could do so much better, my love. And her brother? Don't get me started on him. He's nothing but trouble."

"She's not her brother," I said, bristling in Dakota's defense. Mother turned back to the jewelry cabinet and opened a small drawer. "If you got to know her, you might really like her."

When she turned to face me once more, she held up a small gold ring between thumb and forefinger. Sunlight slanted through the panes of the balcony French doors and glinted off the smooth polished band. It was thin and plain and unlike the elaborate diamond-and-platinum wedding set she wore.

"This belonged to your great-great grandmother. She wore it every day until she died." She took my hand in hers and gently placed the ring in my palm, curling my fingers around it. I stared at my hand, confused. "Don't get any ideas. You're much too young for marriage, but your grandmother wanted you to have this."

A vague recollection of a thin, straight-backed woman with warm hands and a bright smile seeped into my thoughts. My grandmother had passed away before my fifth birthday, but her name conjured the scent of lilacs and the sound of laughter. I gripped the ring tighter and lifted my gaze to meet Mother's. The tinge of sadness in her eyes brought a lump to my throat.

"It was given to her by your grandfather and given to him by his mother. When the time comes, she wanted you to give this to your bride. She said you'd pick a girl who would appreciate it." She moved past me and toward the door, the silk of her dress rustling with each step. "And any girl who didn't appreciate it wasn't worth your time."

The door clicked shut behind her. I held the ring up to see it better. The band was narrow, but a small word was inscribed on the inside, too tiny to read in the dim afternoon light. I thought about the abandoned house on the edge of our property and the hard work of my great-great grandfather to build the fortune of my family. He'd bought many more pieces of jewelry for his wife after he'd acquired his wealth. I'd seen my mother wear them for special occasions, ostentatious rubies and emeralds, decadent diamonds, and the pearl necklace she wore tonight. She'd never wear something so plain, but my great-great grandmother had worn this ring to her dying day when she could've had any ring she desired. Now, it was mine to give to the girl of my choosing.

I shoved the ring into the front pocket of my jeans, guarding the precious reminder from the past, and wondered if Dakota might be that girl.

18

DAKOTA - NOW

IGHT AND AIR filled the interior of the main Seaforth Tower. Glass walls, steel beams, and black marble gleamed around us. From the fourth floor, a mezzanine jutted out over the lobby, filled with people clustered around small tables and drinking coffee. The weight of their curious gazes followed us to the bank of elevators. Samuel made a stunning picture in his suit, the navy blue material contrasting with his sun-streaked hair, emphasizing the width of his shoulders and the narrowness of his hips. He ignored the whispers and stares and concentrated his attention on me. He blinked away when my gaze met his. The elevator tinged, and the doors slid open. The heat of his palm on the small of my back felt familiar and exciting.

Once we boarded the elevator, his touch slid away. He moved to the opposite side of the elevator and resumed thumbing through messages on his phone. When the car stopped at the mezzanine floor, the doors slid open, and Jared MacGruder stepped inside. Samuel continued fiddling through his phone, but I felt the weight of his attention on us.

"Dakota? Is that really you?" Before I could react, Jared pulled me into a hug and dropped a kiss on my cheek, his hand lingering a little too long on my waist.

"Jared. It's been ages. How are you?" I pulled away, a genuine smile on my lips, and tried to ignore Samuel. He'd put away his phone and was now staring pointedly at us.

Jared straightened, looked me over from head to toe, and gave a whistle. "Were you always this hot, or have I just forgotten?"

I laughed and shook my head. Despite his irresponsible ways, Jared exuded boyish charm and playful charisma. He wore skinny blue jeans and a long-sleeved green T-shirt, sleeves pushed up to his elbows. Although he was a nice-looking guy, his casual dress came off sloppy and forgettable next to Sam's power suit.

"We're here to meet with your father," Samuel said.

Jared's head snapped to Samuel, realizing there was someone else in the elevator.

"Jared, this is Samuel Seaforth."

The two men eyed each other. Animosity crackled between them.

"We've met," Jared said after a beat. "Are you working for him now?" He jerked his chin in Sam's direction.

"Yes," I said.

"On a trial basis," Samuel replied. His gaze flicked from me to Jared and back again.

"What's your old man say about that?" Jared asked, a confrontational glitter in his eyes.

"My father doesn't run my life," Samuel replied.

An angry flush spread up Jared's fair complexion.

The tension in the confined space made my stomach

twitter in an unpleasant way. When the elevator stopped at the fiftieth floor, I exhaled in relief and stepped into the hall. Jared lingered at my side, while Samuel glared at us.

"Well, it was great seeing you." Jared dropped a second kiss on my cheek, his hand finding my elbow. He pulled back and smiled. "I don't suppose you'd give me your number?"

Sam's eyes narrowed, cold and assessing, waiting for my answer.

"No, I'm sorry," I said.

"Are you seeing someone?" Jared asked, lifting an eyebrow. He cast a curious sideways glance at Sam. "I didn't mean to step on anyone's toes."

"Oh, we're not together," I said quickly. There was no one and hadn't been for a very long time.

"Then how about Saturday night?" He gave me another smile. I didn't doubt his sincerity. I just wasn't interested in guys like Jared—smooth, reckless, and unfocused. In fact, I'd rather spend the evening alone than in the company of a man who didn't hold my fancy or my respect.

"I really don't have the time for dating," I said. "But thank you for the invitation."

"Well, your loss I suppose." He laughed, unconcerned by my rejection, and touched my elbow again. "Good to see you, Kota." He nodded to Samuel. "Seaforth."

Once Jared turned his back to us, I frowned at Samuel. "You already know him? Why the inquisition then?"

He shrugged and took my arm, leading me toward a set of double doors. "We met at a polo match once."

"Polo?" I lifted an eyebrow. It sounded so atypical for the guy I remembered. "Did you have Grey Poupon while you were there?"

To my surprise, his lips curved in a reluctant smile.

"That was pretty cold, Atwell. You probably bruised his ego beyond repair." Mischief danced in Sam's eyes.

"I don't see the point in pretending I'm interested when I'm not," I said, shrugging. "Life is too short for those kind of complications."

Sam turned to regard me before he pushed open the double doors. Brilliant light erupted. A long sky bridge stretched in front of us, a corridor of glass stretching between the two towers. Even the floor was glass. I came to an abrupt stop, my heart jumping in my chest like a frightened rabbit. Samuel, unaware I'd stopped, continued on another half-dozen steps before he realized I wasn't beside him.

"What?" The question died on his lips. He took a hard look at my face.

I felt the blood drain out of my head. Small black dots danced in my vision. I put a hand on the wall and took a step backward.

"Are you okay?"

"No." I shook my head, focus glued to the transparent floor in front of us and the tiny people moving along the street below. The moisture evaporated from my mouth. I glanced up to his face, desperate for reassurance.

The hardness in his gaze softened. He held out his hand, palm up. "Still scared of heights, huh?"

I nodded and tried to swallow. "I do okay most of the time, but that?" I pointed at the traffic rushing along the street below like toy cars. "That's just scary." I leaned against the wall and closed my eyes.

"You're not budging, are you?"

"No." I heard his deep sigh of exasperation, followed by a sound that might've been a chuckle. I cracked my eyelids, careful to avoid looking at the sky bridge behind him. "Are you laughing at me?"

"Yes." He shoved his hands into his trouser pockets and rocked back on his heels. "So what are we going to do? Do you want me to carry you?"

When he took a step toward me, my eyes flew open wide. He laughed, and I gave him a playful smack on the arm. "Stop it. It's not funny." I placed a hand on my tummy to quell the unrest there. "I'll be fine. Just give me a minute."

"Dakota." The way his voice rasped over my name made me forget the plummeting heights behind him. He extended his hand again and jerked his fingers, beckoning me to accept his grasp. "You trusted me once."

"I know," I whispered.

"I promise it'll be fine," he said softly. Layers of intimacy enriched his words. "I won't fuck with you. Not over this."

Our eyes met. Pleasant warmth replaced the nervous anxiety inside me. Familiar flecks of brown dotted his irises. This was my Samuel, the one I remembered, the one I'd loved. I slid my hand into his. Strong fingers curled around mine.

"Don't look down. Look at me." He stood in front of me, blocking my view of everything but his eyes, his face. He took a step backward, drawing me with him. "Just like old times, right?" I swallowed and nodded and took another step. "Remember your brother's treehouse? I got you up there and you couldn't get down?" His lips curved, revealing the delicious dimples on either side. "It took me hours to convince you to climb up there. You didn't want to but you did it anyway. To please me." I smiled, remembering as he walked me back through time and across the sky bridge simultaneously. "Brave girl."

"You said you'd never been in a treehouse and you wanted to go up there so badly. I couldn't say no." The depths of his eyes swirled with nostalgia and something more—heat, maybe? A flutter rocked my heart. "I could never say no to you."

"Do you remember what we did up there?" Mischief joined the remembrance in his gaze. He was distracting me, forcing me to think about anything other than the scary drop beneath our feet. I played along.

"You know I do." I nodded and bit my lower lip. We'd made love up there with the sun setting in the west, the twitter of birds and the rustle of wind through the leaves surrounding us. It had been perfect and sweet and romantic. Like him.

"I thought we were going to have to call the fire department to get you down," he said, laughter shaking his shoulders. He disconnected his gaze from mine and released my hands when his back hit the door. "There. You made it."

He turned to walk down the hall, and the magnitude of what I'd destroyed hit me like a grand piano dropped from a third-story rooftop. He'd been my everything, my rock, my biggest supporter. I'd thrown it all away, and for what? I still had my brother, but he was on a downward spiral. The money had been spent long ago, and I'd lost something money could never purchase—my self-respect.

DAKOTA - THEN

SINCE MY tryst with Sam, I'd been banned from the Seaforth house. To make up for the loss of income, I worked at the corner convenience store for a few hours once or twice a week. It was pleasant if boring work, running the register and restocking shelves.

Sam and I continued to see each other by stealth. He'd drop me off at the store after school and pick me up at the end of my shift. Rumors swirled around us, but we didn't care. We were in love, and it was no one's business but our own. We were too young and too stupid to know it could never work between us.

I should've known we were on a path of destruction when Mr. Seaforth showed up at the convenience store one night a few weeks before senior graduation. I was sitting outside the store, waiting for Sam to pick me up, when Mr. Seaforth's white Bentley pulled to the curb. He rolled down the window, summoning me to him. I cast a wary glance over my shoulder, suddenly uneasy.

"Sam isn't coming," he said. The ominous tone of his voice sent a chill down my spine.

"I'm sorry?"

"He's grounded for disobeying me once again." The utter disgust in his voice chased away my unease, replacing it with anger on Sam's behalf. "He said you'd be waiting for him and he was worried. I'll take you home."

"That's okay. I'll walk," I said and tightened my sweater around me.

"Wait. We need to talk. About Sam." He leaned across the car and opened the passenger door. "Get in, Dakota."

My gut instinct was to refuse, but some misguided need to defend Sam, to plead our case, spurred me to get into the car. The interior of the car reeked of decadence and power, mirroring its driver. I fastened the seat belt and slid against the door.

"I'll get straight to the point," he said. "I want you out of Sam's life, and I forbid you to see each other anymore."

Being rebellious by nature, the hackles on the back of my neck stiffened. "I don't really think that's your business."

"You're wrong about that. Everything concerning my son is my business." He wore leather driving gloves. They creaked as his fingers tightened around the steering wheel. "He has a bright future ahead of him. He'll be off to Princeton in the fall. What do you think will happen when he leaves? He's going to forget all about you. I don't want to see you get hurt, Dakota."

I didn't for one minute think he gave a shit about my feelings, but he'd hit a tender spot. I knew Sam was leaving. I had enrolled in the local college and planned to live at home, commuting back and forth to school. Neither of us had discussed the impending separation, but it weighed heavily on me.

"If he's leaving in the fall, then you really don't have anything to worry about, do you?" I fidgeted on the soft leather seat, determined to hide my insecurities with a brave face and braver words.

"I don't care to leave things to chance. I see the way you two look at each other. He's obsessed." The tight clenching of his jaw turned my skin cold with apprehension. "Someday he'll inherit everything I've spent a lifetime to achieve. Forgive my bluntness, but a girl of your kind will only slow him down, keep him from attaining the greatness he's destined for."

Tears stung the backs of my eyelids. I blinked them back while my fingers curled into tight fists. No one had ever said anything so deliberately cruel to me before. With one sentence, he'd summed up all of my insecurities and doubts. Sam deserved success, and the last thing I wanted was to stand in his way. I'd always felt a little less, a little different, a little removed from my peers. Mr. Seaforth's words only solidified my burgeoning sense of inadequacy and my doubts.

I could see the lights of my house twinkling at the end of the street, beckoning like a beacon of safety in the distance. Mr. Seaforth slowed the car, prolonging the agony of the drive, when all I could think of was escaping.

"Forgive my bluntness, Mr. Seaforth, but it's Sam's life. I agree he's destined for great things, and nothing you or I say is going to prevent him from it." I gripped the door handle, ready to make my escape the second the car rolled to a stop. "I only want what's best for him and I'd never stand in his way."

He put a hand on my arm, preventing my exit, holding me tightly enough to leave bruises. "What will it take to make you go away, Dakota? Money? I'll write you a check today. With a few calls, you could go to any school you want." His grip squeezed until I wanted to cry out. The weird light in his eyes frightened me. "I can make your life very unpleasant or I can make all your dreams come true. It's your call, Dakota. Which one will it be?"

I yanked my arm from his grasp and bolted out the door. The sidewalk flew beneath my feet as I ran to the house. When I threw open the front door, my mother squeaked in surprise. She'd been knitting on the sofa in front of the TV, her usual place of repose. I streaked past her and into my bedroom, banging the door shut behind me.

Within seconds, she was on my heels. When I didn't answer her knock on the door, she cracked it open. "Dakota? What's wrong? Did you and Sam have a fight?"

"No. I'm fine. We're fine." My voice quavered when I spoke.

She must have heard the panic in my tone because she didn't leave. "Honey, what's wrong? Can I come in?"

"Yes."

In the space of a heartbeat, she was inside the room and holding me in her arms. She hadn't held me this way since I was young. The strength in her embrace undid me. I clung to her, trembling like a leaf in the wind before an impending storm. She rocked me, crooning in my ear, my tower of stability and safety in a world filled with uncertainties.

"My goodness." Her big hand stroked through my hair, soothing and quiet. "It must be something terrible to upset you like this."

She didn't push or pry. It was one of the things I loved most about her, the way she let me come to terms with my anxieties, always patient and loving. When I was able to corral my chaotic thoughts, the words exploded out of me. I told her everything. About Sam. About Mr. Seaforth and his threats. She listened and nodded, her lower lip held tightly between her teeth, blond brows furrowed. After I finished, she sat quietly for a moment, formulating her thoughts before speaking.

"It'll be okay," she said and patted my hand. Her confidence loosened the knots in my stomach. Blue eyes searched my face. "You love him." It wasn't a question, so I didn't answer. A sad smile touched her mouth. "You're growing up so fast." She tucked a loose strand of hair behind my ear with a mother's loving caress. "Everything will work out."

"You don't know that." I buried my face in her shoulder, feeling eight years old again and needing comfort for a scraped knee. Only I was eighteen now, and my problems seemed insurmountable.

"I do know." She pulled back and lifted my chin, forcing me to look at her. The confidence in her eyes soothed my qualms. "Trust me."

DAKOTA - NOW

JOHN MACGRUDER looked much the same as I remembered him, but older, thinner, and more tired. He wasn't much taller than me, with a shiny bald head and a red birthmark above his left eye. When we entered the room, he rose to greet me with a firm handshake and a pleasant smile.

"Come in. Have a seat. Great to see you again, Dakota." He pumped my hand effusively once more. "You've got a good one here, Seaforth." He gave Samuel a shrewd glance. "I hope you're treating her well."

"We've had a bit of an adjustment period, but we're managing," Sam said. Embarrassment heated my cheeks, and I shot Sam a narrow-eyed glare. He didn't smile, but his eyes glittered with suppressed amusement.

Once we were settled around the conference table, I tried to concentrate on the conversation, but my thoughts kept drifting to the color of Sam's eyes, the strength in his hands as he'd led me across the sky bridge, the way I'd felt safe for those brief minutes. There'd been kindness in his eyes and something more, something achingly familiar, before he'd squelched it.

"I've got to admit, your request for a meeting took me by surprise," MacGruder began, jolting me from admiring the square line of Sam's jaw. "I never thought to see you in your father's building."

"It's not my favorite place," Sam said with a nonchalant shrug.

"I have to admit I'm intrigued. It has to be pretty important for you to risk coming here." MacGruder walked to the nearby wall, pressed one of the wood panels, and opened an invisible door. Backlit glass shelves held rows of expensive liquor. He gestured to a bottle of scotch. "Care for a drink?"

"Nothing for me," I said. Although a stiff drink would calm my nerves, I needed to keep my wits about me, still uncertain about my role in this gathering. I cast an assessing glance at Sam, a sense of disappointment filling me. Apparently, the rift with his father remained.

"I'll have whatever you're having," Sam said.

"So spit it out, Seaforth. What do you want?" MacGruder set a cut crystal glass in front of Sam, ice tinkling with the movement. He took a seat beside me, drew a sip from his scotch then clasped his hands on the table in front of him, waiting expectantly.

"I want to buy you out," Sam said.

The expression on MacGruder's face shifted from neutral to wary interest. "Okay. I didn't see that one coming." He laughed. "You've got bigger balls than I thought. What makes you think I'd even consider selling, especially to you?"

"I've got a proposition. One I don't think you can refuse." Sam leaned back in his chair and rested an ankle on his opposing knee. He remained the picture of casual unconcern with the collar of his shirt open, sans tie, but the depths of his gaze held a predatory gleam. My body shifted toward him, drawn by the power of his expression and an ages-old female attraction to an alpha male.

"I'm listening," John said.

"You're between a rock and a hard spot," Sam said. His gaze locked with MacGruder's. I stared, fascinated by the intellectual battle taking place. "You're overextended, growing too fast too quickly. Rumor has it you're a heartbeat away from going under. You've made no secret about your retirement plans. Everyone knows your boys are incompetent. They'll never be able to run this business. You have no choice but to hand over controlling interest to someone more capable."

An uncomfortable flush, reminiscent of Jared's anger in the elevator, crept from MacGruder's collar up his neck and ended in two red patches on his cheeks. His voice remained calm. "That's bullshit. Why would you ever think that?"

"I've got friends all over the city." A cool smile twitched Sam's lips. "You've made a few bad investments in the last year or so. Bought some properties you can't turn around. By my estimate, you're sitting on at least two worthless parcels of land. You counted on my father buying them and when he backed out, he left you holding the bag."

MacGruder's flushed cheeks turned ghostly pale. "What is this? Some kind of conspiracy?"

"Not at all," Sam said. He leaned forward, features earnest. "I'm here to offer you a lifeline."

"You can't afford me." MacGruder shifted in his seat. "I might be in some trouble, but I'm not desperate or stupid." A muscle ticked in his jaw. "You'll need more than insults and observations to win me over. I won't settle for anything less than a fair market price, and frankly, I don't think you have the capital to back up your offer."

Sam eyed MacGruder. The air thickened with tension. I squirmed in my seat, wondering for the tenth time why Sam had invited me to this meeting. My gaze travelled over the aerial photos on the wall of MacGruder's office. Previous acquisitions, I assumed. While the men glared at each other, I stood and walked over to get a closer look at the photos. As I'd told Sam, they were plots of undeveloped farmland, except for the last two. These were interurban areas, the two parcels MacGruder had gotten stuck with. I clasped my hands behind my back and studied the details of the photo, wondering why he would take such a risk.

"That was Jared's idea." MacGruder's voice grumbled near my shoulder. "I gave him free rein to invest in a few properties, and he chose those." He snorted. "I don't know what I was thinking to let him talk me into that." He shook his head and shoved a hand through his thinning hair. "I must be getting senile."

"He can be pretty convincing when he wants to," I said, giving him a sympathetic smile.

"I was hoping he'd convince you to stay with us." John's smile warmed me. I really did enjoy his company, even if his sons were annoying.

"Ansel made me an offer I couldn't refuse. But I enjoyed working for you." I meant every word of it. John had taught me a lot. I turned my attention back to the photos. "What are you going to do with these?"

"I have no idea. Hang on to them, I guess. See if the area recovers. Maybe low-income housing or apartments."

"You said Seaforth senior wanted these?"

"That was the plan." He shrugged and took a resigned gulp of his drink. I felt Sam's ears perk at the turn in conversation. "Bastard backed out at the last minute. Said his interests had shifted."

"What about these?" I moved to another set of photos and tapped on the glass beneath the frame. "Where's this?"

MacGruder shifted to stand beside me. "That is two hundred acres of prime farming ground outside of Cincinnati. Been in my family for a hundred years or so. My grandparents lived there." He used his little finger to trace the outline of the property. "Jared's been after me to sell it."

My gaze met Sam's. He wore a curious look of introspection, as if trying to work out a puzzle whose pieces didn't quite fit.

"If you were to sell the company, would this land in Cincinnati be part of the deal?" I asked.

"I hadn't thought about it. It's not worth much. Not to anyone but me, that is. I don't know why Jared's so hot to sell it." John huffed in exasperation and sank back into his chair. "Like I would listen to anything he has to say after his last debacle."

I scanned the photos one last time, certain I was missing something. The weight of Sam's gaze burned into my back. I resisted the urge to turn and face him, choosing instead to resume my place at John's side. It felt familiar and comfortable to be there, and by John's relaxed posture, he felt the same way.

"You should consider Sam's offer," I said, dropping the volume of my voice to a more personal level. "You always told me that someday you wanted to retire and move away from here. Jared and Junior aren't going to take over. We both know that. This might be the best chance you have to make a clean break. They could keep an interest in the company." Sam lifted an eyebrow at my impertinence. I had no idea what Sam had in mind for MacGruder & Sons. I paused to bolster my confidence then continued. "I'm sure Sam would be flexible in the terms."

"I would," Sam interjected. He leaned back in his chair and lifted his chin, his coat falling open to reveal the snowy-white linen of his dress shirt. "To be frank, John, I think my father backed out on those properties knowing it would put you under. It would allow him to sweep in, acquire the company at a rock-bottom price and all your assets with it. He'd get his land for dirt cheap and make a fool out of you in the process."

MacGruder colored but his eyes shone with respect. "You may be right."

DAKOTA - THEN

IN SPITE of my mother's reassurances, I couldn't sleep after Mr. Seaforth's ultimatum. Blue moonlight streamed through the window of my tiny bedroom and pooled on the bedspread. Through the thin walls of the house trailer, I could hear Crockett in the room next door. The boy slept like he was in a coma and snored with the exuberance of an eighty-year-old man. My mother's footsteps passed my doorway, pausing for an instant, before continuing to her room. I sighed and searched for a more comfortable position on the narrow, lumpy mattress.

Sweat beaded on my forehead. It was only May, and the temperature hovered in the low eighties. The metal walls of the trailer served as an oven, holding in heat from the day. I kicked off the covers and opened the window. Night sounds poured into the room. An amorous cat yowled, frogs trilled in the nearby drainage creek, and the booming voice of Mr. Baker carried on the breeze from the trailer next door. I drew in a lungful of the humid air and tried to still my chaotic thoughts.

"Kota?" At first I thought the whispered call of my

name was a figment of my imagination conjured by the wind. I froze and listened. "Dakota? Are you awake?" This time I heard my name clearly, spoken in a quiet baritone. My body answered with a delicious tingle between my legs.

"Sam? What are you doing?" I sat up in bed and pressed my nose to the screen. He leaned against the side of the trailer, his clean profile outlined by the crisp moonlight against the white siding. "I thought you were grounded."

He held something up in front of the window. An errant moonbeam glinted off the keys to his Porsche. "I had an extra set made." His white smile lit up the darkness. "Rockwell helped me sneak the car to the end of the driveway."

"I love Rockwell," I whispered. "Aren't you worried about getting caught?"

"I wanted to see you," he said. Those five simple words swelled my chest with love. By this time, I knew it couldn't be any other emotion. He pressed a hand against the screen. I melded my palm to his, feeling the heat of his skin through the fine mesh, overcome with longing. "Come out here."

"Are you crazy? It's the middle of the night." I shrank back into the shadows. One look at my face, and he'd know something was wrong. I'd never lied to him before, and I couldn't now. I thought I'd have some time to figure out the answer to my dilemma.

"I'm crazy, alright. Crazy for you," he said. My heart resumed its erratic cadence. How did he manage to turn me inside out with one statement? "Get your ass out here."

We sat on the picnic table at the edge of the yard. Dew lingered on the rough wood surface and seeped into the thin cotton of my pajama bottoms. His fingers eased between mine, curling around the back of my hand. He rested our clasped hands on top of his thigh and stared down at them, the muscles in his neck working as he swallowed. My sweet, beautiful boy. I studied the straight slope of his nose, the curve of his lips, and the proud line of his jaw, marveling for the millionth time that he was my boyfriend.

"Why are you in trouble this time?" I asked, drunk on the endorphins pumping into my veins.

"He forbade me to see you again," he said, his voice rough. His thumb stroked over the back of my hand. "And I told him to forget it. No way."

"He told me the same thing," I said, glumly. "He basically threatened to ruin my life if I didn't break up with you."

We both stared at the ground.

"I'm sorry he's such an ass." The abject unhappiness in his voice made my eyes sting with tears. "He said he'll cut me out completely if I don't break it off with you."

I tried to quell the panic about to submerse me. Over the past few months, he'd become the center of my life. We spent every afternoon and evening together, holding hands, walking around town, stealing kisses. I couldn't imagine my future without him. The idea of losing him hurt more than I realized. My fingers tightened around his until they ached, as if I could somehow keep him in my life by sheer physical force.

"What are you going to do?" The question burned on my tongue. I didn't want to know the answer.

"I told him to go to hell. I don't care about his precious company or the money." With my chin between his thumb and forefinger, he lifted my face until I was forced to look at him. "I just want you, Dakota."

DAKOTA - NOW

AT THE end of our meeting, John MacGruder stood from his chair and shook Sam's hand. He placed an arm around my shoulders and gave me a peck on the cheek. Once all the cards had been played, things moved quickly. John agreed to meet again the next week. Sam sent a quick text to Rockwell, asking him to meet us at the base of the second tower so I wouldn't have to endure the sky bridge again. His unexpected thoughtfulness brought a lump to my throat and added confusion to my already muddled mind. Hate me, he might, but some part of him still cared.

In the hall, Sam turned to regard me. The light of triumph in his eyes gave me more satisfaction than MacGruder's acquiescence. I'd forgotten how good it felt to see him happy. When we reached the elevators, he chucked me under the chin, sending a blast of heat straight through my core and down to my toes.

"You were great in there," he said in his quiet voice. "Perfect." His gaze dipped to my lips. Remembering who and where we were, he stepped back and tugged down the cuffs of his dress shirt in a purely masculine gesture.

"Uh, thank you?" I swallowed. Attraction pulsed through me. This virile, confident Sam had me twisting inside, at war with my better judgment. He had the power to hurt me in a way no one else could. I didn't dare let my guard down for even a second, or these small flashes of kindness might wreck me. "I didn't really do anything."

"You put him at ease. I guarantee he would never have considered my offer without you there."

"Why do you think your father wants to ruin him?"

"Because that's the way he is, Dakota," he said quietly. "When he wants something, he'll go to any lengths to get it. And if he can ruin someone in the process, he'll enjoy it all the more. You of all people should know that."

It wasn't an absolution of my guilt, but it was the closest he'd ever come to admitting his father played a part in our breakup. How much did he know? Had it contributed to their estrangement? I wanted to ask but wasn't ready to open the door to our past quite yet. Instead, I stared at my toes until he touched my arm.

"We should celebrate," he said.

"Celebrate what? The deal isn't done yet."

"We've survived a whole week together and no one has died yet."

Our eyes met. He smiled at me, a full-blown, white-toothed smile, blinding in its beauty. I hadn't seen that smile in a decade. It knocked away my reserve like the shockwave of a bomb. And just like that, there he was. My Sam. The Sam I'd fallen in love with, the only man to ever hold my heart.

I pressed a hand to my stomach, overcome with conflicted emotion. Did I still love him? A wave of disbelief rolled over me. Had I ever stopped loving him? I looked away quickly, seeking control over my thoughts and fluttering pulse. Panic swept through me. Looking for support, I pressed a palm against the wall and scrambled to find my mental equilibrium.

"Are you okay?" The sound of his voice tightened the knots in my stomach.

"Fine. I just need to freshen up a little." I gave him a weak smile and gestured toward the restroom a few feet away.

His gaze flicked to the steel-and-platinum watch on his wrist then up to me. The moment of warmth ended between us as the wall behind his eyes came down. "Hurry up. Rockwell is waiting. I'll meet you downstairs."

The elevator arrived with a ting, and the doors slid open. He stepped inside and left me alone. I went to the ladies' room and took a minute to splash cold water over my wrists and on my neck, not wanting to disturb my makeup. My reflection stared from the mirror in front of me. I stared back, startled by the face I saw. Somewhere beneath the mascara, underneath the designer dress, lurked the girl I'd once been, the girl I'd fought so hard to obliterate. What did Sam see when he looked at me? Certainly not the girl he'd married or loved.

Move on, Dakota. I could no more afford to be in love with Sam than I could afford to walk away from my contract. To do so would be personal and professional suicide. If I was still in love with him, I needed to hide it from the both of us. My emotional and financial welfare depended upon it. Out of a need for self-preservation, I did the only thing I could do. I locked all my emotions into the closet of my soul, and threw away the key.

Once I'd made the decision to ignore emotion, a

comforting calm descended over me, numbing me. I touched up my lipstick, forced a brittle smile of acceptance onto my face, and walked out of the restroom. I tapped a quick text to Sam, telling him I was on my way, and turned my attention to the number display above the doors, showing the elevator descending from the top of the building.

Any consolation I'd felt was short-lived when the elevator doors opened and the cold, calculating gaze of Maxwell Seaforth stared back at me.

23

DAKOTA - NOW

I RESISTED the instinctive need to flee in the opposite direction. Two men in suits stood at my elbow, briefcases clutched at their sides. They moved around me to step on the elevator car, murmuring hushed greetings to Mr. Seaforth. He hit the open button for the doors, his gaze leveling on me with the intensity of an undetonated bomb.

"Take another one," he told the men without looking at them.

I stepped backward, intending to wait for the next elevator as the men debarked. The look of panic on their faces would've been comical under other circumstances.

"Not you," he said, his voice holding the same command I remembered from my youth. "I want to talk to you."

"I've got nothing to say to you," I answered, surprised by the amount of control and confidence in my voice.

"Well, I've got something to say to you, and if you're smart, you'll hear it."

The spurned men stared at me wide-eyed and disbelieving. I studied the man in front of me, weighing the sanity of accepting his proposal. I'd forgotten the similarity between son and father. Both were tall and broad-shouldered, carrying an undeniable air of command. The similarity ended there.

"Dakota." Mr. Seaforth barked my name, his voice sharp and laden with animosity.

I narrowed my gaze on him and lifted my chin to let him know I wasn't intimidated. Once I'd boarded the elevator, the doors slid shut. The air became close. I faced forward, refusing to look at him. "Whatever you've got to say, say it," I said. "Because it will be your only chance."

He grabbed my elbow. I shot him a look of pure hatred. He withdrew his hand with a small noise of amusement. "I had to see it for myself. I couldn't believe it. That he'd have anything to do with you." The contempt in his voice shriveled my insides. It was arctic cold, his disgust matching mine. "After what you did—"

"You mean after what *we* did." I turned to face him. We stared at each other. This man represented everything I hated about myself. It was like standing next to the devil, whispering temptations into my ear, daring to lead me down the path to ruin and damnation. I clutched the phone in my hand tighter. It vibrated with what I assumed was Sam's answering text. I glanced down at the screen, unseeing. "Excuse me," I said, my tone dripping with fake politeness. "It's your son." I pretended to tap out a quick text, but I turned on the video recorder instead and dropped my hand to my side. I didn't trust this man.

"Why is he here?" he asked, eyes searching my face. "I want to know everything." He took a menacing step toward me. "You *will* tell me everything."

I snorted contemptuously. "Hell if I will. If you want

answers, ask him yourself." I resisted the urge to glance at the floor numbers, wishing the damn elevator would hurry. It was fast, but not fast enough.

"I wonder what he's up to," he mused. The weight of his gaze pinned me to the floor. "How's your mother, by the way? And your brother? I hear Crockett is up to his old tricks." The veiled threat in his inquiry had my hands trembling, but damn if I'd give him the satisfaction of showing it.

"You've been checking up on me?" The gall of this man baffled me. "Why are you so threatened?"

His laughter seared my ears. "You're no threat. He hates you more than he hates me."

"Thanks to you," I replied.

"If you're in the picture again, there has to be a good reason, and I want to know why." He sneered down his nose at me. "How much will it cost?" He drew his wallet from his pocket. "I don't have much cash on me."

"To hell with you and your money. I'm not a naïve kid anymore," I said, unable to contain my temper any longer. "You can take your wallet and shove—"

The elevator doors slid open at the thirty-seventh floor, stopping me mid-insult, and a cluster of young, pretty women stepped inside the car. Their gazes flicked from me to Mr. Seaforth. The tension between us was palpable, even to them. We rode in uncomfortable silence to the lobby. His fingers found my elbow once again, pinning me to his side until the others had left.

He leaned close, the heat of his body chilling me from the inside out. "You'll be back."

I yanked my arm from his grasp and squared my shoulders. "Don't count on it."

I sprinted through the lobby and out the door. Sam stood beside the car, phone to his ear. Our eyes met and a furrow formed between his brows. I tried to school my features into nonchalance. Seeing his father left me empty and chaotic. The recording of our encounter sat in my pocket like a loaded gun. I wasn't sure what to do with it, but having it gave me a small sense of reassurance.

24

SAMUEL - NOW

DAKOTA PUSHED through the revolving doors of the tower and exploded out onto the sidewalk, a harried light in her eyes. I stood beside the car, cell phone at my ear, with Tucker on the other end of the line. A burst of wind caught the hem of Dakota's dress and swirled it above her knees. At the sight of her stockings and garter straps, my conversation stumbled. I'd always been more of a breast man, but knowing she wore sexy lingerie beneath her dress captivated my imagination, derailed my focus, and tied my tongue.

"Sam?" Tuck, spoke my name for a second time. "You still there?"

"Yes. Let me call you back."

"Sounds important." Tuck's lazy voice always held a note of laughter. Now was no exception.

"It is." My gaze locked on Dakota's face. She was pale, her eyes huge and round. Alarms sounded in my subconscious. I'd seen that expression before, years earlier. Foreboding tightened my chest.

"Don't forget we're having drinks after the fundraiser thing. You got a date yet?" he asked.

"Sure," I said, even though I hadn't given one thought to the event. The takeover of Harmony, Dakota, and the business with MacGruder had kept my mind preoccupied.

"Liar." Tuck knew me too well and called me on it. "You've got two weeks. And remember, if you show up dateless, you owe five thousand bucks to the charity of my choice. And Dahlia doesn't count."

"You really don't like Dahlia, do you?" Rockwell moved to open the door for Dakota, but I waved him away and opened it myself. She stopped and glanced over her shoulder, like she expected someone to be following her.

"No. I don't trust her, and you shouldn't either." I heard Tuck's words but couldn't pry my eyes away from the strange expression on Dakota's face.

"Look, this is urgent. I'll catch you later." I ended the call and dropped my phone into my pocket. If Tuck knew the urgent matter was my ex-wife, he'd give me a truckload of well-deserved shit. Being a lifelong bachelor himself, he had no understanding of commitment or monogamy or the devastation of ending a relationship.

She slid into the car. I followed behind her. We drove in silence down the street for a few minutes. I scrolled through my work email, unable to focus on anything besides her withdrawal. Her introspection confused me and tempered some of my elation over MacGruder. Part of me wanted to ask about her mood; the rest remained stoic and silent. I didn't want to know or care about whatever issues she wrestled. Emotional entanglement would only put my heart at risk, a mistake I'd never, ever repeat with her.

Guilt washed through me as I shot a sideways glance at her. She looked miserable, and I could hardly blame her.

Exhaustion tempered my mood. Executing vendettas was tiresome work. Maybe I'd been a little harsher with her than she deserved. Sure, she'd done me wrong, but it had been over a decade ago. What kind of petty jerk held on to a grudge for so long? My father. The realization filled me with so much self-disgust that my fingers clenched into fists. This was the way he acted, toying with people's emotions, playing with their lives like characters in a video game.

On impulse, I leaned forward, tapped Rockwell on the shoulder, and murmured new instructions in his ear. He nodded and changed our route. Dakota and I needed a reprieve from our silly game. I hoped, with a little effort, we could reach some kind of neutral ground. I'd loved her once and spurned my father to have her. She'd felt the same way, at least in the beginning. Despite my constant denials, I was dying to know what made her stop.

When the car halted outside Gabriel's Landing, Dakota glanced up at me, confusion plain on her features. "What is this?"

"I thought we'd have dinner," I said. "I know you're hungry. I can still hear your stomach pitching a fit. You never got to finish your lunch." I don't know why it suddenly seemed so important for me to feed her, but it did. Maybe I wanted to show off a little, impress her with how far I'd come in life. Maybe it was because I'd never been able to afford a swanky restaurant when we were married. Either way, I wasn't going to take no for an answer. She opened her mouth to speak, a frown of refusal on her face. I shook my head in warning. She shrugged, and I felt the tiniest bit of disappointment when she didn't argue.

We ate dinner in uncomfortable silence. I ordered enough food for four people along with a bottle of their most expensive cabernet. She picked at her food and didn't even notice the wine, except to refill her glass twice. Her lack of recognition left me dissatisfied. I wanted to rub my success in her face, to show her what she'd given up by forsaking me, goad her into admitting she'd made a mistake in leaving me.

"Have you been here before?" I asked, wanting to break her insufferable silence. Even when she was quiet, she pissed me off. At least when she spoke, I had her attention.

"No." She lifted the bottle of wine and poured the last drop into her glass. "It's a little swank for my taste."

"Do you like the cabernet? It's an exclusive vintage. We're lucky to get it."

"Oh?" She tilted the glass and took a gulp. "I hadn't noticed." I frowned, and the corners of her mouth curved. "Of course, as far as I'm concerned there are only three types of wine. Cork, screw top, and box." She took one last drink, draining it. "So if you're trying to impress me, it's a waste of your time and money." Her tongue swept over her lower lip with sensual slowness. I glanced up to her eyes and found them full of playful light. My incorrigible girl was back again.

"Really? I thought you'd swoon at the absurd cost of this bottle." I gripped it around the neck and held it up for her inspection. "So what does it take to impress you these days? Cars? I've got six. Houses? I have two."

"Only two?" She ran a finger around the rim of her wineglass. "So materialistic, Mr. Seaforth. I'm disappointed. You always hated people who bragged about their wealth."

A wave of heat rushed up my neck and into my face. I heard my father's voice, recounting his assets, prizing wealth above all else. I scowled to cover my irritation. "I'm not bragging. I'm stating facts. Life is about chasing what you want and grabbing it with both hands. And I always get what I want these days."

"And what is it you want?" She stared at me, her focus roaming from my eyes to my lips and back to my eyes again. That simple act made my cock stiffen. I'd never felt so seen before, not before Dakota, and certainly not since. I shifted in my chair.

"I want it all. Everything." Beneath the table, my knee grazed hers. Sparks of attraction skittered up my leg and into my groin. "I want to prove to my father that he was wrong about me." I let my leg rest against hers. She didn't pull away. "What do you want, Dakota?"

"To be happy." Her answer came quickly and without consideration.

"That's it?" I sat back in the seat and tried to school the surprise off my face. Most girls when posed with this question would recount endless lists of clothes and cars and houses, but Dakota wasn't most girls and never had been.

"Isn't that enough?" she asked.

It wasn't enough for you, I thought, but held the statement back. If she didn't want money, why did she leave me? The question had kept me awake every night for the past week. "Of course, being a millionaire in your own right probably raises the stakes a little," I continued. Her face darkened, and I felt a surge of triumph. I'd hit a tender spot. If she was angry with me, she wasn't ignoring me. Being male and an ass, I poked a little more. "What are your minimum criteria for a date these days?"

"You might be surprised," she retorted.

We moved to the bar following our meal. I followed behind her, unable to tear my eyes from the swing of her ass beneath that silly little dress. I'd had a few drinks myself by this time. The heat and warmth of the alcohol moved through my veins and loosened my tongue. We slid into a dimly lit corner booth.

"I'll have a Sun King," I told the bartender.

"And what will the lady have?" The bartender turned to her, a flirtatious smile on his lips.

"I'll have a martini," she replied.

"You look like the kind of girl who likes it extra dirty," he said, giving her a wink.

My fingers curled with the urge to give him a taste of my fist.

"The dirtier, the better." She smiled at him, parting pink lips. Jealousy rumbled through my veins, burning and molten-hot. I wasn't sure what bothered me the most—knowing another man wanted her or knowing I couldn't have her. Either way, I didn't like it. Even though I had no intention of being with her, I wanted her to want me. The bartender's gaze connected with mine, and the smile slipped from his face.

"Was that absolutely necessary?" I asked her when he'd left.

"Probably not. But I enjoyed it anyway." She cast a flirtatious glance at the bartender, who smiled at her from behind the bar. Her blue gaze blinked back to me. "Not everyone hates me, Mr. Seaforth."

"Is that the kind of guy you go for now?" I asked. She confused me at every turn. I couldn't imagine her wasting time on a man without a hefty income. Her gaze flitted to my mouth again, and my cock responded by thickening. At this rate, I wouldn't be able to leave the booth for a good long while.

"He's cute. I'd do him." She regarded the bartender, trading smiles with him once more. I smoldered in my seat.

When her focus returned to my face, a mix of relief and tension heated my chest. "You're better looking."

"But that's not enough for you," I replied. What I really meant was that it hadn't been enough for her to stay married to me. The need to understand why she'd left me overwhelmed my thoughts. I said I didn't care, but I did. Her rejection had fueled every corporate takeover and every one-night stand over the past ten years. I'd done it all to prove her and my father wrong. I'd made a success out of myself without my father's help, but it still wasn't enough.

"It was never about your looks or your money, Sam," she said in a small voice.

We stared at each other for a long minute. She took in every detail of my lips, nose, and eyes. Having her undivided attention felt better than I cared to admit. Once, I had been the sole focus of her life. I missed that kind of devotion. These days no one gave a shit about my existence. Most women only wanted into my bed or my bank account. My mother had passed away a few years ago. My father dedicated his life to ruining mine. My sister, Vanessa, had married a French diplomat and moved to Paris. Aside from Tucker and Beckett, there was no one.

"If you met me at a bar, would you try to pick me up?" I asked.

She lifted an eyebrow. "As long as you didn't speak." She was teasing. A glimmer of our former playful camaraderie shimmered over me. "Would you hit on me?"

I let my gaze rover over her. Hell, yeah, I'd hit on her. She'd let her hair down. Long, chestnut waves swept over her shoulders. Her breasts taunted me, high and round and full. Were her nipples still pink like rosebuds? I used to love the way they'd tighten when I circled them with my tongue. Reading my thoughts, a blush swept up her neck and into her cheeks. She swallowed and ran her tongue over her lower lip. The action sent my cock into full alert. I was completely hard by this time, and she'd done nothing more than look at me. I exhaled a long sigh. I was so fucked.

"Yeah. I would," I replied, and shifted to relieve the pressure behind my zipper. She affected me in a way no other woman ever had. The fine threads of attraction still stretched between us, dangerous as a spider's web. Was it knowing she was unattainable that piqued my need to have her? Or a need to show her what she'd given up?

"Would you take me to a hotel?" she asked. Her voice was low and husky, too familiar. I knew that tone and what it meant, where it would lead. I followed, heedless of the risk. "Or would you want to do it here?"

"Either." I swallowed against the constriction in my throat. "Both." A vision of her pressed against the wall, breasts flat against my chest, one of her legs wrapped around my waist, sent a zing of need straight into my groin. Her gaze locked onto mine. "I'd fuck you so hard you wouldn't know your name afterward."

"I'm wet just thinking about it."

I searched her face for signs of teasing, but her eyes were dark and somber. Neither of us was playing around now. This was serious talk. I became hyperaware of her as a woman. The rise and fall of her breasts. The heady scent of her perfume, sweet and fresh. The subtle shift of her body when I leaned toward her, acting and reacting in response to each other. I wanted her more than anything, but hell would freeze over before I let her reject me again. She needed to come to me this time.

"Show me." My voice sounded rough to my ears, barely more than a whisper, but she heard it. Now I knew what I wanted. I wanted to control her, bend her to my will, make her obey.

Her hand took mine beneath the table and guided it along the inside of her thigh, over the elastic band of her stocking, and up the strap of her garter belt. When I felt the brush of neatly trimmed pubic hair, my cock twitched. Sweet bleeding Jesus. The girl was going commando. Lust buzzed in my head. She nudged the tip of my finger inside her folds, where she was slick and wet.

"Damn," I rasped. Our gazes remained locked. Years of longing and hurt danced back and forth between us. In my head, she'd been a mixture of fantasy and nightmare. With the tantalizing heat of her wrapped around my fingers, the present washed away the past. All I could think about was controlling her and making her yearn for me. Before I was through, she'd beg for it, and once she acquiesced, I'd reject her, the way she'd rejected me.

At this inopportune moment, the bartender returned with our drinks. Seeing my glare, he wisely kept silent and returned to his station. Dakota ran a fingertip around the rim of her glass, a smart-ass smirk on her face, unaware of my plan. The smirk disappeared when I slipped a finger inside her. Her eyes went wide with surprise. I brushed my thumb over her clit, making slow, tiny circles. She bit her lower lip until it turned white around her teeth.

"I bet I could make you come like this. Right here," I said, my imagination piqued by the challenge.

"You wouldn't," she said on an exhale. I could tell the idea excited her, though. Every time my thumb made a circle, her pupils grew wider, and her nostrils flared. "Are you crazy? Someone might see."

"No one can see. Besides, they're not interested in us." The bar was well made with tall dividers between each booth. Our booth had curtains draped around the perimeter, shielding us from the patrons on either side.

"Maybe I'm not interested," she said. Her statement ended in a little gasp as I teased her with my fingers.

"You still want me." I studied her face, the high color in her cheeks, and the tremble of her hand resting on the table, more turned on than I'd been in years. She'd always had that effect on me. A decade later, nothing had changed.

"I never stopped wanting you." Her hand migrated to my fly and squeezed my length. "It was never about not wanting you."

"No." I shook my head. I needed to stay in control and couldn't with her touching me. She moved her hand away, obedient for the first time all week. She liked my game. I was in control now, and the knowledge sent a heady rush of triumph surging through me.

We both had one hand above the table and one below. While my right hand teased her, she gripped the top of my thigh with her left. I took a drink of my beer but kept my gaze on her face, enjoying the way she fought for control of her expression. She couldn't control her eyes, however. The faster my fingers moved inside her, the wilder the light in her eyes became. Her chest lifted and fell, each breath a struggle. Her nails bit into the muscle of my leg. I couldn't look away, fascinated by the way she responded to my touch. I'd wanted control over her, and I had it now.

"Sam." She spoke my name, a soft whisper, her voice cracking on the single syllable. I felt her tighten around my fingers. Her legs twitched and her body tensed as she came. The ripples of her orgasm shot up my arm. I held her gaze with mine, daring her to look away. She didn't. In the hazy depths of her eyes, I saw vulnerability and regret intertwined with need. She drew one shuddering gasp and leaned back in the seat. I'd meant to break her, but in that moment, with my fingers slick from her desire, I couldn't bring myself to do it.

Rockwell dropped us at her apartment building. I told him to wait fifteen minutes, and if he didn't hear from me, to leave and I'd catch a cab. He had the good grace not to smirk when I told him this. I followed Dakota into the elevator and to her door. We were both a little drunk from too much liquor and from each other. Inebriation gave me courage and overrode my common sense. It was the only excuse I could come up with for what I was about to do.

I stood inside the entry of her apartment and waited while she went to tidy the bedroom. I studied every square foot with curious interest. The furniture was adequate but nothing special. The whole place was no bigger than a postage stamp. Hell, my bedroom closet was larger. I'd felt big and awkward as a teenager, my six feet four inches dwarfing the small space. I'd expected something grander, stuffed with expensive décor. After all, she had a million dollars to her name, and I was paying her a decent salary.

This peek into her private life jumbled my preconceived opinions. Where had all the money gone? I raked a hand through my hair before shrugging out of my suit jacket and slinging it over the chair. She'd never been an impulsive spender when we'd been married. To the contrary, she'd counted every penny, clipped coupons, and made an art out of thrift. Her clothes were nice but not ostentatious. Maybe she'd travelled around the world or had a secret drug habit. No, I knew better. She was too smart for drugs and too scared of flying for world travel.

By the time she reappeared, I'd managed to school the

confusion off my face. She held out a hand. I took it, mesmerized by the haunted depths of her large eyes. We didn't speak as she pulled me into her bedroom. It was barely big enough to hold the bed. I had to turn sideways to fit between the mattress and the wall.

"What am I doing here?" I asked, voice cracking on the words. It had been easy to push away reason when my dick was hard, but now I wasn't so confident. A million doubts surfaced in my muddled brain. All I could think about were the dozens of ways she'd wrecked me, the potential ways she might hurt me again. I watched her kick off her shoes, eyes glued to mine, and licked my dry lips. She could only hurt me if I cared, which I didn't. Did I?

"I want you, Sam." She pulled her dress over her head, revealing a satin bra and matching garter belt, nothing else. My memories of her body paled next to the real thing. She was toned but curvy in all the right places, heavy breasts straining against the cups of her bra. My cock began to harden again, eager to feel the wet heat of her. She tossed the dress on the floor and climbed onto the mattress, kneeling in front of me.

"Don't talk," she said, and pressed a finger to my lips. "Just let me do this." Her fingers flew over the placket of my shirt, releasing the buttons with practiced speed. The familiarity of the act made my stomach drop.

"I thought you didn't fuck your bosses." I couldn't help throwing her words back at her, giving her a chance to back out before we went too far.

"You're not my boss right now," she said. Her face tilted to mine, brow furrowing. "We're Sam and Kota. We were married."

The weight of her words settled around my shoulders. *We were married.* Not friends, not lovers, but husband and wife. The permanence of our relationship went deep, and the roots of it still tangled in the depths of my soul. *Till death do us part.* She hadn't meant the words when she'd said them, but I had. Divorce might have legally separated us, but the court system had failed to evict her from my soul.

"I don't trust you." My voice scratched my throat. I felt raw and vulnerable, like she'd peeled away my skin.

"It's alright. I understand." She smiled up at me, her eyes brighter than usual, even in the dim bedroom. "You may never trust me again. I don't deserve that honor. But for one night, let's forget about the mess of our past." She pushed the shirt over my shoulders and slid her palms over my pecs. When her fingers reached the waistband of my pants to tug on my belt, her request made perfect sense. I could do that—forget for tonight—*just* tonight. Once again, we were in the same headspace. "I want to taste you, Sam, feel you inside me. It was always good between us. We were good at this."

The way her gaze flew to mine, full of question and needing reassurance, gave me instant amnesia. I forgot about my insatiable desire for revenge and control. Her hand slipped inside my boxers and gripped my cock. I groaned and bent my head to find her mouth. All I wanted was to bury myself inside her and remind her she was mine.

25

DAKOTA - NOW

A DECADE of fantasies was nothing compared to the reality of Sam. He stretched out on the bed, one arm tucked behind his head, fully naked in front of me. His gorgeous green eyes were hooded, sheltering his thoughts. The smooth, tanned stretch of his torso beneath my fingers sent jolts of electricity up my arms. A smattering of gold hair trailed from his navel down to his long, thick cock. He was lean and toned from neck to toes, a blond Adonis in my bed, erect and ready for the taking.

Before now, we'd been playing with each other. This seemed much more serious and not at all inconsequential. We were treading on treacherous ground. Chances were good that one of us would leave this bedroom wounded and battle-scarred. I knew without a doubt it would be me.

Strange how I played it safe in life with everything but my heart. I always looked twice before crossing the street. I double-checked the locks on my door before bed each night. I balanced my checking account daily. When it came to Sam, however, I tossed my heart around like a volley ball, heedless of where it might land.

A dull, sweet ache throbbed between my legs at the sight of him. I trailed a hand over the ripples of his abdomen, savoring the warmth of his skin beneath my touch, the woodsy scent of his cologne. He seemed familiar in the best possible way. Once, I'd known his body better than my own. He had changed subtly, grown leaner and more taut, broader and harder. I straddled his legs, wearing nothing but my stockings, garters, and bra. His eyes travelled over me, growing darker and more heated, sending a shiver of anticipation down my back.

"Take your bra off," he commanded in a scratchy voice. His palms rested on my thighs, warm and large. "I want to see your tits." I reached behind my back to undo the hooks. "But you can leave these on." He slipped a finger beneath one of the garter straps and tugged. "These are sexy." When he let go, the band snapped against my skin.

The straps of my bra slid down my arms. I felt shy and uncertain, like I was eighteen again and it was our first time. I needed to know he wasn't going to cut me down at the last minute or laugh at my efforts. My nipples tightened into painful peaks when the open air hit them. His eyes met mine. Any qualms I had drifted away at the appreciation in their depths. He couldn't fake that.

"You're beautiful, Kota." He cupped each breast in his palms, weighing them, and brushed his thumbs over the tips. When he sat up and sucked a nipple into his mouth, I trembled at the sensation of heat and wet and suction. "I've missed these."

His words broke me in an entirely new way. I pulled his face up to mine and took his mouth. Our kisses were sloppy and hurried, as if we were trying to devour each other. He wrapped his arms around my waist and pulled me against him. The length of his cock nestled into the apex of my thighs. I ground my hips against him, overcome with the need to have him inside me.

In one fluid motion, he flipped me onto my back and settled between my legs, spreading my knees wide with his. I understood his need to take control and relinquished it willingly. I had wounded his ego, stripped him of the power in our relationship, and broken his heart in the process. If he needed to take the steering wheel, I'd be a willing passenger if it meant one more night together.

I fumbled in the top drawer of my nightstand for a condom. He held the base of his erection with one hand, while I rolled the thin sheath over the tip and smoothed it down his shaft. Our harsh exhalations broke the silence. We'd done this a hundred times before, but it had never felt so new, so raw, so different. We weren't kids anymore, weren't married, and this wasn't going anywhere past tonight.

His gaze lifted to meet mine. Emotions tangled inside me, knotting and twisting around each other. How many times had I dreamed of this? How many times had I awakened during the night, damp with sweat, quivering from post-orgasmic release, only to realize the bed beside me was empty? I devoured the sight of him, taking in every angle and plane of his cheeks, the straight line of his nose, and the strong angle of his jaw. I felt famished, devastated by insatiable hunger for him. Just him. Only him.

His eyes darkened, taking in my reaction. When I was a kid, Crockett and I had done somersaults down a hill in the park, turning over and over and over in a dizzying dive to the bottom. I felt the same way now, disoriented, plummeting down without heed to direction or destination, tumbling headlong into the unknown abyss of Samuel Seaforth.

He grabbed my hip and shoved into me—deep, commanding, and proprietary. A startled breath hissed between my lips, like steam escaping from a boiling kettle. Fire spread through my veins and into the farthest reaches of my limbs, consuming me. He was a match to my gasoline, the catalyst to my destruction. When he drew out and slid inside me for the second time, I came in a violent shudder, ripples of agonizing pleasure coursing along my legs.

"Sam." I whispered his name.

"That's right," he growled. "You're going to take me, Dakota. All of me. Every inch." He drew back again and slammed into me. Our skin slapped together with each of his punishing thrusts. "This is payback for every sleepless night you ever gave me."

"Yes," I answered and drew my nails down his back, reveling in the primal tone of his voice. "Punish me. Make me pay."

Every slam of his pelvis pushed my body further up the mattress. He wrapped an arm around my waist and lifted me, angling into me deeper, holding me to him. I could do nothing more than cling to his back while he rode me. His quiet grunts of pleasure sang in my ears. I'd never wanted anything more. I prayed for it to be over, I prayed it would never end, and I prayed he wouldn't see how much I needed his touch.

When his release shuddered through him, a masculine growl rumbled through his chest. I caressed his back, soothing the scratches left by my nails. He rolled off me and threw a forearm over his face, shielding his expression from me. The second his body left mine, emptiness filled me. Time had dulled the ache of his absence, but with him lying next to me, the heat of his body burning down my side, I couldn't deny I'd missed him any longer.

We lay motionless, side by side, the sound of my pulse pounding in my ears, darkness around us. A dozen times, I opened my mouth to speak, but words eluded me. Would he get up and leave now? Was this it? How would I ever face him at work, knowing I meant nothing to him while he meant everything to me? He had always meant everything to me.

Following an eternity of silence, he moved over me again. The full weight of his body pinned me to the mattress. I struggled to see his expression in the dim light, but his eyes were heavy-lidded, sheltering his thoughts. When his hand went to the nightstand for another condom, a bevy of butterflies fluttered in my stomach.

He braced an arm on either side of my shoulders, holding his chest well above me. One heartbeat then two before he slid inside me, slowly and gently. A solitary tear oozed from the corner of my eye and slipped onto the pillow. He withdrew and entered me again, savoring the sensation. A wavering sigh escaped my lips. His soft kiss in the hollow above my collarbone filled me with euphoria.

Each long, unhurried stroke of his cock tore away a piece of the wall around my heart. This was Sam making love to me, the way he had when we were married, the way it used to be. I didn't deserve his kindness or his tenderness, but he was giving it to me anyway. I had the feeling he could no more help himself than I could help loving him.

"You should never have left me," he said.

"I know," I replied. When his eyes met mine, filled with fire and longing, I knew it would never be over for me.

26

SAMUEL - NOW

DAKOTA SIGHED and shifted beside me. The first rays of morning streamed into the room, shades of gray and lavender and pink bathing the walls with warmth. I turned to face her. My bones felt liquid, dissolved by our marathon of sex. Sleep gave the curves of her face an angelic sweetness. I traced a fingertip over the slope of her upturned nose before dropping a kiss on her mouth.

"Sam," she whispered, not waking.

The sound of my name on her lips wrung my heart. I turned away from her, swinging my feet onto the floor, and passed a hand across my forehead. I felt weak, exhausted by the emotional back and forth. What began as a revenge fuck had turned into lovemaking, more powerful than any in my experience.

I moved silently about the room to retrieve my clothes. With my back to Dakota, I put on my trousers and shirt, fingers stumbling over the buttons. This had been a huge mistake. I'd wanted to put her in her place, to steal from her everything she'd stolen from me: her self-respect, her happiness, her power over me. All I'd succeeded in doing was opening a door to the past that refused to stay closed and deepening the gash in my heart.

I found my phone in my jacket pocket and called a cab. Rockwell was probably up, but I didn't want to face him. One look into my eyes, and he'd see the turmoil inside me. I just wasn't up for that kind of scrutiny, not until I'd had time to sort out my feelings.

Once dressed, I turned to her for the final time. She had rolled onto her back. The sheet puddled around her waist, exposing her breasts and the smooth column of her neck. Asleep, she looked young and vulnerable, the ghost of the girl I'd married. I swallowed down the lump in my throat, chasing away a tangle of longing and regret. Whatever we'd had together still existed. I'd felt it in the brush of her fingers over my back, the softness of her lips on mine, and the way her body had spasmed around me with each of her climaxes.

I moved to cover her, tugging the cotton sheet up to her shoulders. Something fell from the bed onto the floor at my feet, landing with a light plink in the pre-dawn silence. I glanced down. A glimmer of gold winked by my shoe. I bent to retrieve it and lifted it into the air.

At the end of a delicate gold chain hung the thin circlet of my great-great grandmother's wedding band. My heart stopped beating. I recognized the chain as the one Dakota wore to work every day. How many times had I seen her fingering the necklace while she spoke, all the while unaware of what it held? One of the links had broken, presumably during our sexcapades, and it had slipped from her neck.

I clutched the necklace in my hand until my knuckles ached from the strain. After all this time, she'd kept the ring. I'd given it to her along with my heart, and she'd never returned either one after the divorce. I'd wondered about the ring from time to time over the years but always shoved the thoughts away, unable to endure them for more than the briefest of seconds.

On the bed, Dakota stirred. I panicked and shoved the ring into my pocket before hurrying out the door. I couldn't face her. Not now. Maybe not ever. There were too many questions cluttering my thoughts and too many emotions warring inside me. Why would she wear the ring every day if I meant so little to her? Why did I care? Why did the vision of my ring nestled between her breasts over the past ten years make me want to wake her and make love to her all over again?

Jesus. I raced out of the apartment and, after pressing the elevator call button a dozen times, opted to take the stairs. I plunged down the steps two at a time. The taxi arrived in front of the building as I exited the door.

"Where we going?" the cabbie asked, eyeing me through the rearview mirror.

I raked a hand through my hair, uncertain of my destination. All I knew was that I needed to get as far away from Dakota as possible before I charged back up the steps and demanded an explanation from her.

"Twenty-first and Elm," I said, giving the address of my home office. It was the only place I could think to go under duress. At least I'd be alone there on a Saturday morning. I needed time to think, to sort out my feelings, and try to make sense of the chaos. Last night, I'd made love to my ex-wife. She still wore my wedding ring. I still had feelings for her. Hell, I'd never lost my feelings for her. They'd only been dormant, awakened by her presence. If I was to have any peace of mind, I needed to exorcise her from my soul. Somehow, I knew that was never going to happen.

27

DAKOTA - NOW

I AWOKE mid-morning on Saturday, hovering between dreams and wakefulness. For the briefest of moments, disoriented by the best sleep I'd had in years, I thought Sam and I were still married. I swept a hand over the cool sheets, searching for him. He liked to rise early, while I liked to sleep late. I stretched, enjoying the delicious ache of the aftermath of good sex, before opening my eyes and remembering. A wave of nervous dread chased away the fog in my head.

"Sam?" I sat up, listening for sounds of him. Only the tick-tock of the alarm clock on the dresser and the bark of a neighborhood dog greeted me. Maybe I'd dreamed the whole thing. I rubbed the grit from my eyes, once again feeling the pull of muscles tested by strenuous sex.

The previous day and night came flooding back to me. The meeting with MacGruder. Dinner at Gabriel's Landing. Sam between my legs, broad shoulders looming over me as he brought me to release over and over and over. I hadn't imagined any of it. Desolation filled the spaces between my ribs until I thought my chest might burst. Even though he hated me, he'd made love to me. I covered my face with my hands, unable to face the truth of my emotion. I still loved him. I'd never stopped loving him.

Of course, he'd left. Why would I expect anything else? I meant nothing to him. Our night together had been an exorcism meant to erase me from his soul. Had he succeeded?

On instinct, my fingers went to my neck, seeking the gold chain and my wedding band. It wasn't there. I jumped from the bed and tossed the pillows to the floor. I never took the necklace off, except to shower. What if Sam had seen it? Would he be angry? I yanked the bedclothes from the mattress and shook the sheets, desperate to find it. I crawled on the floor, searched beneath the bed, and retraced my steps through the apartment, but the necklace was nowhere to be found.

During my frantic hunt, I glanced at the clock and saw it was past nine. I had a brunch date with my mom. We had a standing appointment once a month. Usually, I looked forward to spending time with her, but today, a ripple of anxiety replaced my anticipation. A glance in the bathroom mirror revealed the events of the previous night lined my face. Worried shadows circled my eyes, and no amount of makeup would cover them.

After a hasty shower, I arrived at the diner on time. One look at my face, and Mother knew something was wrong. Being a paragon of patience, she waited until I finished my second cup of coffee before broaching the subject.

"Are you going to tell me about Sam, or do I have to drag it out of you?" she asked finally.

"You know?"

She nodded. "Crockett told me."

"Traitor," I grumbled. Eager to change the subject, I said, "I saw Rockwell the other day."

A warm light brightened her eyes in a way I hadn't seen for many years. "Rockwell? That sly devil. Where did you see him?"

"He's still driving Sam around." I hesitated over Sam's name. Speaking of him with my mother seemed too familiar and too painful.

"Tell him I said hello, will you?"

"Sure."

We fell silent for a minute.

"Sam. How is he?" To cushion the importance of her question, she took a biscuit from the basket and began to slather butter on it.

"He's fine," I said, couching my expression with caution. "Different. The same. Infuriating."

"Too much salt," she said after a bite of her biscuit. I recognized the telltale scrunch of her face as she analyzed the ingredients, and I smiled in spite of my distress. Once a chef, always a chef. "Are you two getting along?"

"Not really." I sighed and dropped my fork onto the plate, abandoning any idea of eating. "He hates me."

"Can you blame him?" She met my gaze with the honesty I cherished. "Did you expect anything less, Dakota?" Although her words were tinged with kindness, the truth from her lips hurt me more than I could admit.

"I did a terrible thing, didn't I?" Tears stung my eyes. I tried to blink them away, but this time one escaped and rolled down my nose. "Why didn't you stop me?"

"By the time I knew what you'd done, it was too late. And you'd already made up your mind, hadn't you?" She reached across the table to cover my hand with her large one, roughened and reddened by years in the kitchen. "Yes, you did a terrible thing."

Overcome with emotion, I made a move to leave the booth, but her hand tightened on mine, demanding my surrender. I needed to get out of here before I completely broke down, but she wasn't going to let me go unless I made a scene. We'd never discussed the details of my divorce, and I didn't want to now.

"No, Dakota." Her hand held me firmly in place. "I never said anything before. It was your life and your mistake to make. But I'm going to say my piece, and you're going to listen." The wood bench bit into my back, hard and unyielding like her grip. "I know how much you loved him, baby, and it broke my heart to see what you did." I lowered my head, filled with shame. "That doesn't mean I love you any less. You did what you thought you had to do. I don't know your reasons, but I stood by you, and I still do."

I covered my face with my hands. "I messed up, Mom. I ruined the best thing that ever happened to me. I don't know what to do." She must have heard the break in my voice. Before I knew it, she was on my side of the booth, pulling me into her strong arms and holding me the way she had so many years ago.

"You make it right, baby. And you forgive yourself. You can't keep punishing yourself for something that's already done." The clean scent of her soap mingled with the lingering smell of bread, comforting me. "Do the right thing this time, Dakota. I'm so proud of you for becoming such a strong woman. You'll do what you need to do."

By the time I arrived home, I had several text messages and two missed calls from Muriel. Too unsettled by my ethical and emotional dilemmas, I decided to delay calling her until later. Instead, I grabbed a cold beer from the fridge and plopped my butt onto the couch to try and get my head straight. Mom was right as always. The past couldn't be repaired, and I would have to live with my mistakes. The future, however, was under my control.

The phone rang again. Muriel's face splashed across the display. "OMG, you never give up," I said by way of greeting. "This better be an emergency."

"It *is* an emergency," she said. "I have to go out tonight."

"No way." I propped my feet on the coffee table and took a long pull off my beer. "I'm done in, Muriel. I need a break."

"Exactly," she said, voice shrill with enthusiasm. "We're hitting a nightspot. Somewhere exciting. You can't say no."

"I can and I just did," I replied.

"Dakota!" She moaned in consternation. "You never go out anymore. What happened to the fun-loving girl I used to know?"

"Muriel." I tapped the phone against my forehead in resignation. "Okay. Fine. But I get to choose the place."

"Perfect. As long as there are hot men there."

She arrived at my apartment a little after nine, took one look at me, and narrowed her eyes. She swept her gaze from my head to my toes and lifted an eyebrow. I shifted the unruly mass of my hair over my shoulder, while a blush heated my cheeks. She circled me like a hungry vulture. "You got laid last night."

"You're crazy," I said and tossed a lipstick into my purse. "We'd better get downstairs. The taxi will be here any second."

"I need to get laid," she said with a dramatic sigh while we waited on the sidewalk. The taxi sped into view, tires squealing around the corner and onto my street. "It's been forever."

"How was your interview with Dahlia?" I asked, eager to change the subject. Muriel had been nervous about sitting face to face with the bitch-troll.

"I think it went really well. She seemed interested. Said there are lots of opportunities with Infinity for someone like me." The broad smile on her face warmed me. "I think I might get a promotion."

I squealed and threw my arms around her. "Muriel! That's fantastic. Why didn't you tell me?" The taxi slid to a stop in front of us. "We have to celebrate." In spite of my own dilemmas, I was truly happy for her. Sam had come through for her, and I felt a small rush of gratitude toward him.

"I'm telling you now." She beamed at me, opened the car door, and hopped inside. I followed after her. "So, who's been slipping you the salami?"

I flushed again, remembering the feel of Sam inside me, the scent of his cologne, and the warmth of his skin against mine. "No one."

"I suppose you gave yourself that hickey." She crossed her arms over her lap and sat back in the seat with a satisfied smirk.

"I burned myself with the flat iron," I said and looked away so she wouldn't see the lie on my face. I couldn't talk about it, not yet. It was too personal and still too fresh in my mind. I wanted to keep the memory safe. Speaking about it might fracture the fragile bubble of my sanity.

"Okay, if that's the way you want to play it," she said with a shrug.

"Where to?" the driver asked, and I gave him the name of the first place that came to my lips.

I didn't think Felony Bar was what Muriel had in mind, but that was where we went. Her eyes grew round when our taxi turned down a street lined with debris and graffiti-covered, rundown buildings. She gripped my arm tightly when I led her down the alley to the entrance of the underground club.

"Really?" she asked in her most pretentious voice. "Do I need my mace?"

"Maybe," I said. With every step further into the building, my mood plummeted a notch. I didn't want to be here. I needed to be home, beneath my mother's afghan and with a good book, where I was safe. I had too many things to mull over, none of which I could resolve at Felony.

"This is exciting," Muriel whispered. "I feel really naughty."

I laughed in spite of my mood. The rusty steel door creaked when I gave it a shove and led her down the dark hallway. Fog from smoke machines swirled around our feet, lending an eerie vibe to an already creepy place. A tall, muscular guy with biceps the size of my thighs met us at the dance floor.

"You got IDs?" he asked in a deep, raspy voice. We dug in our purses then held up the requisite identification for his perusal. He took a hard look at our faces then handed back the cards. "Go ahead, ladies. Enjoy."

As we walked away, Muriel turned to watch the guy walk away. "I'm not usually into redheads," she said, fanning herself with a hand, "but I could make an exception for him."

"Are you in heat or something?" I asked, not even attempting to hide my irritation. Everything rubbed me the wrong way. It was like wearing a wool sweater with nothing under it. Every comment or gesture from every living thing poked at me.

"At least I'm not an icicle," Muriel huffed, and I immediately regretted my harsh remark.

"I'm sorry." We pushed our way to the bar through a sea of people clad in black. Some wore multiple piercings in their face. Others had colored hair. Some had both. "I told you I was in a bad mood."

Two stools opened up at the bar, and we slid into them before anyone else could take them over. The band started up, playing a cover of a Slipknot song. I leaned over the counter and spied Jack at the opposite end, radiating more hotness than seemed humanly possible. When he looked up from pouring a draft beer, I waved. He jerked his chin in response, collected payment from his customer then sauntered over to us.

"Hey, you made it," he said. His chocolate brown eyes roved over my scoop-neck tank dress appreciatively. By the time his gaze made it to Muriel, she was ready to swoon. "Who's your friend?"

"Muriel, Jack. Jack, Muriel." I heard her choke on a gasp, and I really couldn't blame her. He wore a white wifebeater T-shirt, exposing the rounded muscles of his shoulders. Tattoo sleeves covered his arms. The tight cotton of his shirt clung to the ripples of his abdomen.

"Pleasure, Muriel," he said, flashing her a smile made of pure sex and dimples.

"Um," she replied.

"What can I get you, ladies?" He tapped a hand on the counter and returned his attention to me.

"Um," Muriel said again.

I rolled my eyes. "I'll have a Crown and Coke. She'll

have a vodka tonic. And bring us a couple of Jaeger Bombs, would you?"

"Coming up," he said.

I watched him go to work, admiring the play of his muscles as he moved behind the bar. He was hot in a bad boy kind of way, something I used to go for, but now I couldn't help comparing him to Sam. I gave him a twenty-dollar bill and told him to keep the change. He winked and went back to work.

The music was good but not great. The drinks were better than average. After a while, Muriel relaxed and ventured out onto the dance floor with a guy named Heath. I sat on my barstool, pounding down the cocktails and thinking about my options.

The crowd thickened. The music grew heavier and darker. Muriel vanished in the sea of bouncing bodies. I watched Jack at the end of the bar, thinking he might provide the distraction I needed, but his attention was focused on another girl, someone I recognized. When he returned to refill my drink, I couldn't resist asking him, "Who's that girl over there? I think I know her."

He blinked up at me from the bottle of Crown Royale in his hand. "What girl?"

"The one with all the curves and the dark blond hair." Not wanting to be conspicuous, I jerked my head in her general vicinity. "You know, the one you've been staring at through your throng of groupies?"

Dimples flashed from either side of his devilish smile. "Oh, that's Ally Taylor."

I repeated the name, rolling the syllables over my tongue, searching the recesses of my memories. I shook my head. "Maybe not." I returned his smile. "You like her?"

He shrugged. "She's got a boyfriend. I don't think she even knows I exist."

In spite of my funk, I laughed. "Jack, I'm pretty sure she knows you're here. So does every other female within a fifty-mile radius." He didn't reply, just winked and moved back to the other end of the bar.

The smile slid from my face when I spied Crockett standing near the dance floor, surrounded by his worthless friends. He wore a leather vest over tattered blue jeans and a black T-shirt. He'd spiked his hair into a Mohawk and colored the tips burnt orange. While I sipped on my cocktail, I watched him disappear a dozen or more times into the men's room with various other people. A knot of disappointment tightened in my chest. I knew without a doubt he was in trouble again, back to selling drugs.

I'd just gathered my resolve to confront him when the bouncer, the one who'd greeted us earlier, began to stalk across the floor from the other side of the room, his gaze homing in on Crockett like a predator. The crowd parted for him with uneasy sidelong glances. I caught a glimpse of Jack in my peripheral vision. The mischievous sparkle in his eyes was replaced by something darker and more frightening. He reached beneath the bar, but Crockett drew my attention again.

A guy wearing black lipstick and multiple piercings in his ears pushed Crockett, and Crockett shoved him back. A brief but incendiary conversation ensued between the two men. The music was too loud and the distance too great to make out what was being said, but their body language left no doubt. I'd seen Crockett angry a time or two in my lifetime. I slid off my barstool, intending to defuse the situation, but it was too late. Crockett popped the guy in the mouth. In the space of a second, all hell broke loose.

Jack jumped over the bar, baseball bat in hand, and charged at the melee. The bouncer shoved through the crowd with impressive speed. By this time, Crockett and his adversary were rolling on the floor, knocking over tables, and throwing punches. The band stopped playing. The meaty smack of fists on flesh filled the silence.

Within minutes, it was all over. Jack wrestled Crockett to the floor and pressed a knee to his back to hold him down. The bouncer grabbed his opponent by the neck and slammed his head onto a table. Two uniformed cops arrived. My heart hammered against my ribs. I pushed through the gawkers, but by the time I reached Crockett, he was already handcuffed.

"You need to step back, Miss," the officer said. He held Crockett by the arm and extended a hand to ward me away.

"He's my brother," I said. "I'm willing to vouch for him."

Crockett refused to look at me. He stared across the room. Blood trickled from one corner of his mouth. A purple knot began to rise above his left eye.

"You can pick him up at the station," the cop said. He yanked Crockett toward the exit. "He's got an outstanding warrant. You can sort things out there."

My hopes plummeted. Not only was Crockett on probation, he had an outstanding warrant as well, something he'd failed to share with me. I scanned the room, searching for Muriel. I needed to call a bondsman and Crockett's attorney right away. Otherwise, he'd have to spend the weekend.

As my focus roved over the cluster of leather-clad, pierced, and tattooed onlookers, my gaze met Jack's. He wiped the back of his hand across his mouth, showing the pink tinge of blood on his lips.

"Sorry, Dakota," he said. "But he's had it coming. He's been dealing drugs in here for months now, and I just can't have that shit going on here anymore."

My cheeks burned with embarrassment. "It's okay, Jack." I spied Muriel at a booth and turned toward her, but Jack stopped me with a touch of his hand to my arm.

"He's in some deep shit," he said. "The people he's working for don't play around. Maybe you should leave him in jail for a while. Let him think about what he's doing."

I stared at Jack. The thought of leaving Crockett to his own devices had never occurred to me. The idea made my guts ache. He was my family, my baby brother. All my life, I'd worried over him. Mom had said once that I treated him more like my own son than she did. I suppose it was from all the years I spent babysitting him while she was at work.

"What kind of sister lets her brother sit in jail?"

"The kind who doesn't put up with shit like that," Jack retorted without missing a beat.

Jack's words stayed with me long after I returned home. The more I thought about Crockett's situation, the angrier I became. Not just with him but with myself for putting up with his irresponsibility over the years. How many times had I bailed him out? The offenses continued to escalate in severity. Each time he promised to change, and each time he disappointed me. He wasn't a kid anymore. He was an adult, and so was I.

When the county jail's number flashed across the caller ID of my phone, I turned the ringer to mute and went to bed. Thunder rumbled outside my apartment. I tossed and turned, troubled by disturbing dreams of Crockett and Sam and Mr. Seaforth. Sometime around dawn, I glanced at the phone and saw a voice mail from my mother. I called her back immediately, fully awake, fear gripping me. The last time she'd called this early had been to tell me she was in the hospital.

"Crockett's in jail," she said without preamble.

"I know."

"We need to call the bondsman. Can you pick me up, and we'll ride over there together?" I heard her flurried movements, as if she was gathering her things into her purse.

The little shit had called Mom. She didn't need this kind of stress with her weak heart. A renewed wave of anger swept over me at his selfishness. "I don't think we should, Mom. Not this time."

"I'm not asking you to bail him out. He's not your problem to solve." She exhaled into the phone. "I've got a little money put back. Maybe I can get a loan."

"Mom, no." I closed my eyes, overcome by weariness.

"I can't leave him in there." The dismay in her voice sent a wave of guilt through me.

"Mom, we're not helping him." I'd bailed him out time and again, keeping it secret from her, afraid her weakened heart couldn't withstand the strain of the truth. In her eyes, Crockett was still the frail, sweet-natured baby boy of my childhood. "I don't see the point in bailing him out when he's so determined to go back in. Maybe he needs a little time to think about the consequences of his actions. This morning you said I needed to take responsibility for what I'd done and make things right. Crockett needs to learn that lesson, too."

She was silent for a long moment. I heard a chair scrape across the floor. I pictured her taking a seat, presumably at the dining room table. When she finally spoke, her voice wavered with weariness. "He was such a sickly child, coming down with every childhood illness. I don't think we missed a week without a visit to the doctor or the hospital until he was ten."

"He's a big boy now, Mom." I felt her pain through the phone. "He needs to know he can't keep doing this kind of thing. It's like every time we bail him out, we're giving him permission to do it again."

She murmured something unintelligible, the sound thick with tears. "I did the best I could for the two of you. It was hard without your father. He needed a man in his life, but I just couldn't bring myself to date again after your dad died." Tears of empathy pricked my eyes. "I relied on you too much, leaving you two alone when I should've been there."

"Mom, you did a great job. The way Crockett is—it's not a reflection on you." I cupped the phone to my ear, wishing I could reach through the phone and give her a reassuring hug. She meant so much to me. She'd been my rock and salvation when I might have crumbled. Crockett had no idea how lucky he was to have her.

"You were always the strong one, Dakota," she said, sending a surge of love radiating through me.

After I hung up the phone, I didn't feel like the strong one. The threads holding my sanity together were about to snap from the strain. I closed my eyes and rested my head in my hands. When I opened them a few minutes later, the first light of day filtered in gray and pink beams through the blinds of my bedroom window. A day had passed since Sam had taken me to bed, but I felt like I'd aged a year.

After a brief phone call to the jail for details about Crockett's situation, I met with him. He was allowed a fifteen-minute visitation. It broke my heart to see him wearing handcuffs and a neon orange jumpsuit. He sat across the table from me, refusing to meet my gaze as if I was the one who'd disappointed him and not the other way around.

"How long until you can get me out of here?" he asked, sullen gaze trained on the far side of the room.

"I can't get you out this time," I said, steeling myself for his anger.

"Can't or won't?"

"Both." An uncomfortable beat passed. "Your bail is super high. I don't have enough money to get you out." It wasn't a lie. I'd been living from paycheck to paycheck for the last year. Any spare cash went to support my mother. By the time I paid rent, there was little left for anything else.

His knee bounced up and down, belying his frustration, and he ran a hand through his unkempt hair. "What about Mom? Can she help?"

"Leave Mom out of this, Crockett. You know she doesn't have any money." My voice rose, buoyed by anger. "She agreed that you need to stay in here for the time being."

"What about the condo? She can put it up as collateral."

"No." I slammed a hand on the table between us. The guard narrowed his eyes, and I sat back. "You selfish little shit," I hissed. "I'm so mad at you, Crockett. You promised to straighten up after the last time."

He hung his head and studied his hands resting in his lap. "You've got no right to judge me." The amount of self-righteous anger in his voice stiffened my spine. He'd never spoken to me like this.

"I've got every right," I said, barely holding my temper in check. "I'm the one who's paid your lawyers and the fines. You have no idea what I've sacrificed to keep you out of trouble, and you don't appreciate any of it." Blood thundered through my head, making my temples pound. "You're twenty-six years old. Mom didn't raise you to act like this."

"You think you're so much better than me with your fancy job and your education. We both know you didn't get where you are by following the rules." His face scrunched up the same way it had when he was seven, and he didn't get his way. "You and I are the same, Kota. We're just playing different games."

I sat back in my chair, wounded by his accusations. Everything I'd done had been for his benefit, and he wasn't the least bit grateful. The realization put my efforts into perspective. Life was all about making choices. I'd made bad choices for good reasons. The best I could do was to learn from my mistakes and do better. It was a lesson Crockett seemed unable to comprehend and one I'd prevented him from learning.

"Time," the guard said. He stepped toward Crockett and twirled a finger in the air. "Wrap it up."

Crockett stood. "I can't believe you're going to leave me here." He changed tactics and managed to look contrite. "Come on, Dakota. Please help me."

At his pleading words, my eyes blurred with tears. I watched the guard lead him away. He looked small and scared, a ghost of the fragile little boy he'd once been. As he walked through the steel door and disappeared, I tried to remember that I wasn't responsible for his poor decisions, nor was he responsible for mine. I'd divorced Sam to save Crockett, but I'd only ruined us all. Maybe if I'd let Crockett face the consequences of stealing Mrs. Seaforth's jewels, he wouldn't be here now. I stood and walked out of the jail, leaving my baby brother behind. Next to leaving Sam, it was the hardest thing I'd ever done.

28

DAKOTA - NOW

A MISTY rain shrouded the city as I entered the building on Monday. I arrived late, following a dentist appointment, feeling the trajectory of my life had forever been altered by the events of the weekend. Butterflies whirled in my stomach at the thought of seeing Sam. I had no idea how he felt about our tryst. I could only assume by the way he'd left my apartment in secret that the encounter had meant nothing to him, while it had meant everything to me. With a sigh of resolve, I squared my shoulders and prepared to do battle. My heart might be broken, but innate strength flowed through my veins and shored up the tattered walls of my defenses. I'd been through a lot in my twenty-nine years, and I wasn't about to give up now. If I did, it would mean all my efforts had been in vain.

Muriel brushed past me as I closed up my umbrella, clutching a cardboard box in her hands. Tears streaked her cheeks. Two building security officers flanked her side. She was so intent on leaving that she didn't even notice me. I scurried after her, concerned, and touched her arm before she reached the revolving door.

"Muriel? What's wrong?" She turned to face me with red-rimmed eyes. I saw the items in her box—a framed photograph of her cat, a wilted ivy plant, and a plaque. "Oh my God."

"I got let go." She sniffed. "Reduction in workforce, they said."

"No. That can't be right." Muriel played an integral part of the marketing team and her work had always been above par. No one in their right mind would let her go.

"Please, Ms. Atwell," said one of the security guards. "We have instructions to escort Ms. Green off the property."

"I'm so sorry," I said to Muriel. She smiled through her distress, brave soul that she was. "Call you later?"

"It's okay. I'll be fine." With a resolute squaring of her shoulders, she pushed through the revolving door and disappeared into the cityscape beyond.

When I entered the reception area of Harmony Enterprises, an eerie silence prevailed instead of the usual friendly banter. As I walked along the aisle to my cubicle, a few pale faces glanced up from computer monitors. A dozen or more desks sat empty. No one spoke. I went straight to Sam's office, bypassing Valerie completely. She opened and closed her mouth like a landed fish sucking in air but let me pass. I knocked twice on the door and entered uninvited.

Dahlia sat on the corner of his desk facing Sam. She wore a tight red skirt with a slit up the side, revealing a slender stretch of calf and a trim ankle. Her left hand rested on his shoulder. Their laughter ended abruptly when I opened the door. Sam had been smiling, the full-lipped, white-toothed smile that always made my chest squeeze. He used to smile at me with the same brightness. It faded when his eyes caught mine. My stomach did a triple flip at the sight of him.

"Can I speak to you a minute, Sam—I mean, Mr. Seaforth?"

Dahlia's eyes narrowed at the familiar address. Her gaze swept over my white suit, the navy ruffled blouse and my blue-and-white spectator pumps. I'd put extra care into my outfit that morning and, by the catty gleam in her eyes, had chosen well.

"We were in the middle of something," Dahlia said. She stood and straightened her skirt with a tug on the side seams.

"It's fine," Sam said. "We're done here." Her brow furrowed, and I felt the smallest kernel of satisfaction in her pique at being dismissed. "What is it, Ms. Atwell?"

I waited until she'd shut the door behind her before I spoke. "I met Muriel downstairs. She said you canned her. What's going on?"

He clasped his hands on the desk in front of him. His eyes met mine without a hint of expression in them. The warmth from the weekend had chilled. I had done that to him. I had taken away the heat and laughter from his life. Had he managed to exorcise me at long last? Sadness mitigated some of my anger over the whole Muriel situation.

"We had to let a few people go today. It shouldn't come as any surprise. I was up front about the merger from the beginning." The tight line of his jaw suggested he expected a fight. I curled my fingers at the memory of the scratch of his stubble over my belly when he'd kissed me there.

"I understand the logistics of the situation. I saw Muriel in the lobby. She's always been a valuable asset. I hope you were fair about it." Although he didn't extend an invitation to sit, I took the chair in front of his desk anyway. Sexual tension crackled through the air between us like static electricity.

"You're worried about her?" The stubborn set of his shoulders eased.

"She's a good person. Of course I'm worried." Our gazes collided and held. A dull ache of need throbbed between my legs at the sight of his moss-colored eyes.

"More than fair, Kota. Everyone got a severance package in line with their years of service, as well as access to job placement resources. I can assure you no one was left high and dry." I opened my mouth to speak again, but he stopped me with a raised hand. "And your friend Muriel was given the opportunity to interview at one of my satellite offices, if she's interested."

I exhaled a sigh of relief. "Thank you. I appreciate that." When he didn't say anything more, continuing to stare at me, I stood to leave.

"Is that it?" he asked, disbelieving.

"I believe so," I said. We stared at each other, a thousand wordless conversations passing between us. I searched his eyes, desperate for a hint of his thoughts. His face was cold, expressionless, and sober. I decided to throw myself over the cliff. What the hell. He already hated me. Our relationship was fucked up beyond description. I had nothing left to lose. "Unless you want to talk about Friday night?"

One of his broad shoulders lifted in a nonchalant shrug. "We were drunk. We fucked. Nothing else to say, is there?"

"No. I guess not." I gave him a polite smile as the space between us widened into a yawning chasm.

My hand gripped the door handle before he spoke again. "I want to meet with you about MacGruder tomorrow at ten. And bring me everything you can find on his property in Cincinnati."

I nodded but didn't turn around. "Is that it?"

"No. I gave Valerie a list of errands. See that you get them done before the end of the day. That's all. You can go now."

Armed with Sam's credit card, I stared at the list in my hand, disbelieving. There were at least twenty-five items. It wasn't the list that irked me as much as the detail he'd put into each item. One red silk necktie with blue-and-gold stripes. Two bottles of absinthe from France. A leather-bound unabridged copy of *The Catcher in the Rye*. I bit my lower lip, contemplating the items. This wasn't a dismissal. The bastard had picked up our game without missing a beat. I scanned over the items one more time, a thrill of adrenalin racing through me at the challenge. A glimmer of hope buoyed my deflated spirits.

On the sidewalk outside the office building, I hailed a cab and dialed the number of a friend who owned an exclusive bookstore on the north side. It took six hours, but I managed to obtain every item on the list, including the absinthe, courtesy of Jack. The challenge kept my mind occupied, away from thoughts of Crockett and Mr. Seaforth and Sam. Before returning to work, I made a quick stop at a high-end lingerie store to purchase a new pink satin garter belt. The thought of Sam's expression when he saw the lingerie on his credit card statement brought a smirk to my lips.

I enlisted the help of a security guard to carry the items back to Sam's office. I dumped them on his desk at five forty-five and dusted my hands together in front of him. "Anything else?" I asked.

He cast a cursory glance at the myriad shopping bags

and boxes but didn't look at me. "Did you get the information on Cincinnati?"

"I'm working on it," I said.

"Okay," was all he said before turning his attention back to his laptop screen.

"That's it? Not a thank you or good job or anything?" I asked, disappointed. "I worked my ass off and you have to admit, it wasn't an easy list."

He sighed and closed his laptop before turning to face me. "What do you want me to say, Dakota?"

All my pent-up emotions exploded at once. "I don't know. Something. Anything." I waved my hands in the air. "How can you just sit there and act like nothing happened between us Friday night? Are you that kind of guy now?"

He lifted his eyebrows and sat back in his chair, considering me. "What do you mean, *that kind of guy?*"

"The kind of guy who makes love to his ex-wife then leaves without saying goodbye or any kind of acknowledgment? Really, Sam?"

He leaned further back in his chair, widening the distance between us. "Honestly, I didn't know what to say."

I wanted to stop talking before I embarrassed myself further, but the words kept pouring out, beyond my control. "It wasn't just sex, Sam. We made love." I slapped my hand onto his desk, causing his pen to roll over the edge and onto the floor. "You made love to me." One corner of his mouth twitched, but I wasn't sure if from amusement or irritation. Either way, I was just getting started. "And these stupid lists." I picked up the piece of paper and flagged it in the air. "Oh, my God. I'm sick of your lists." With a dramatic flourish, I tore the paper in half then proceeded to shred it into tiny bits. They rained to the floor like confetti.

A knock sounded on the door. Valerie peeked her head into the office. "Is everything okay in here?"

Sam cleared his throat, tearing his eyes from mine. "It's fine, Mrs. Wayne. We're fine." Laughter shook his voice. "Ms. Atwell was just having a temper tantrum. I think she's done now."

With a groan of exasperation and embarrassment, I gathered my dignity and stomped past Valerie. I paused at my desk long enough to collect my purse and briefcase before leaving.

29

SAMUEL - NOW

THE NEXT morning, the sight of Dakota at her desk made my pulse pound like a schoolboy. It was only a few minutes after seven. The other employees wouldn't arrive until nine, yet here she was, plugging away at her computer. Her tenacity and willpower never ceased to surprise me. Whenever life threw an obstacle in her way, she climbed it and squared up for the next challenge.

"Good morning, Ms. Atwell," I said, and smiled at her answering grunt. She'd never been a morning person. "Are you ready for our meeting?"

"I have until eleven," she said in a strange voice.

I still wasn't sure what to make of her. Being near her elicited thoughts and feelings I didn't want to face, but after our lovemaking, I could no longer ignore them. Part of me wanted to strangle her for throwing away our marriage, while the other part wanted to mend her broken pieces and make her love me again. It was a foolish notion, but one I couldn't push aside. She was as much a part of me as the blood in my veins.

Anger flooded through me at my inability to control my desire. "Make it ten," I snapped.

"Sam," she whispered. Every time she said my name, it tore me apart. It was the reason I wanted her to call me Mr. Seaforth, which I normally detested. "Can you just give it a rest? I've had a hard couple of days."

"Don't tell me you're still upset about yesterday?" I put a hand on her chair and swiveled it around so she was facing me. She stared to the side, avoiding eye contact, but I could see her eyes were red-rimmed and swollen, like she'd been crying. Her hand went to her neck, and I knew instinctively she was looking for the gold chain, the one in my front pants pocket. My resolve to be an asshole wavered.

"Don't flatter yourself. I'm fine," she said. Her chin jutted stubbornly. "I was up all night working on this. I'm just tired."

"Fine," I said.

"Fine," she repeated.

I turned and strode to my office without a backward glance and slammed the door for good measure. Her face continued to haunt me throughout my meetings and conference calls. I was angry, but more with myself than her. Why did I still let her get under my skin? After all this time, I should have learned my lesson. Maybe my father was right. Maybe I was just stupid where she was concerned. The more I thought about it, the angrier I became until I'd worked myself into a tempest by the time of our meeting.

I needed to put her in her place. She'd fucked me over, and hell would freeze over before I let it happen again. I was Samuel Seaforth. I'd crushed companies and brought the owners to their knees in front of me. I could do the same with Dakota. Fuck her contract. She needed to go before I let her ruin me. I'd make her so miserable, she'd beg to quit. One way or the other, I would win.

At precisely ten o'clock, Valerie announced Dakota. She knocked on the door before entering. She strode into the room wearing a dark green blazer, matching skirt, and a white blouse, the picture of confidence and capability. My heart kicked against my ribs. I squashed the buzz of attraction like a pesky mosquito. There would be none of that today. This was a duel to the death.

"Are you ready?" she asked, her voice controlled.

"Yes." I stood and moved to the conference table.

She took a seat across from me. All traces of strife had been erased from her face. I watched her lay out a dozen reports across the surface of the table, mesmerized by her quiet efficiency. "I think you'll be pleased with what I've found," she said.

"I'd better be," I replied, baiting her.

Her gaze lifted to meet mine. The absence of emotion in her eyes chilled me to the core. Disappointment bowled over me. She was gone. My sweet, stubborn Dakota had evacuated the premises and left behind a capable automaton. "I've got all the information you requested on the Cincinnati property as well as the surrounding areas," she said in a flat tone.

My attention drifted as she cited statistics and demographics. I searched her face, filled with unexpected panic. Had I gone too far? Had I finally pushed her to the breaking point? Until this point, I hadn't realized how much I enjoyed the friction of our relationship. Now I suddenly, desperately wanted it back.

"Stop." I placed my hand over hers, halting her mid-sentence.

"Is something wrong?" she asked, lifting her gaze to mine.

"Come here." I curled my fingers around her hand.

"No." The point of her chin quivered. Stubbornness flashed in her eyes. Relief loosened the knot in my stomach.

"Dakota. Get the fuck over here." I tightened my grip on her hand, drawing her around the end of the table to stand in front of me.

She stared up at my face, jaw clenched and lips pressed into a tight white line. "What?" Her blue-green eyes met mine. I saw determination and an unbreakable spirit staring back at me. My knees dissolved with relief. Fuck me, I loved that look. She wasn't broken. I hadn't broken her. My father hadn't broken her. She was too strong and too obstinate to crumble.

"Nothing," I said and drew her into my embrace.

She rested her cheek against my shoulder, her body unyielding, her arms rigid at her sides. I placed a hand on the back of her head and held her there until the tension drained from her shoulders. The scent of her shampoo wafted up to me. I bent and buried my nose in her hair, savoring the fragrance of citrus and honey. We stood that way for a long time.

"This is screwed up," she said, her voice muffled in my shirt. She slipped her arms inside my jacket and around my waist.

"Pretty much," I replied and rested my chin on the top of her head, enjoying the way she fit there like she belonged. The way her body molded to mine left me undone. This was so much more than I'd bargained for and not at all what I'd had in mind as an outcome.

"You're making me insane." Her voice reverberated into my chest.

"I really want to hate you." I brushed my lips over her hair. "It would be so much simpler that way."

She sighed. "I know. I get it."

When she turned her face up to mine, chin resting on my sternum, my resolve dissipated. The solid feel of her in my arms washed away the hatred and left me wanting for more. Before I could give voice to my feelings, she pushed me back and straightened her clothing. Her small smile carried a tinge of sadness.

"Let's get back to work," she said in a voice edged with steel.

She returned to her seat and tapped one of the graphs. I watched her walk away, taking the heat of her body with her, leaving me empty and alone on the opposite side of the table. It always amazed me, the way she could dismiss me without so much as a backward glance. The rejection stung. Once again, I remembered all the reasons I wanted her out of my life.

"I've seen enough," I said. She frowned but began to gather the documents. "Leave them. We're done."

"Um, okay." She stood and paced to the door like her skirt was on fire.

Once the door closed behind her, I slid into the chair behind my desk and straightened my tie, more determined than ever to put an end to this madness. As soon as the MacGruder deal was settled, I'd offer her a nice severance package and send her on her way. Ansel would just have to understand.

30

DAKOTA - NOW

B Y WEDNESDAY, I was a quivering mass of indecision. Part of me looked forward to working with Sam. Sitting across the conference table from him gave me a thrill to the tips of my toes. Another smaller part of me wanted to curl up in a corner and cry. We'd had something good and wholesome and wonderful between us once. Little glimmers of it shone through the cracks of our relationship now and then, teasing and taunting me.

I knew for certain I couldn't continue this charade for long. No matter how much I tried to deny it, I still loved him. I'd always loved him and always would. It was just the way I was made, to only love one person, and that person was Sam. I didn't understand the man he'd become, but it didn't matter, not really. We were both different people now, but he would always be the one for me.

Being around him was sheer torture. Every time he passed by my desk, the tiny hairs on my arms and neck lifted. The sound of his deep voice sent jolts of desire along my synapses. The few times we happened to brush against each other in passing caused my insides to clench in the most delicious way. I had no idea if he felt the attraction the way I did. If the glower on his face was any indication, the answer was no.

We had a meeting with MacGruder after lunch. Because Sam had a prior meeting elsewhere, I arrived at Seaforth Towers alone and met him at MacGruder's office. We didn't speak directly to each other for the duration of the meeting. Afterward, we rode the elevator to the lobby in uncomfortable silence, standing on opposite sides of the car to avoid touching each other.

Fearing another altercation with Sam's father, I kept glancing over my shoulder, certain he'd snatch me into a corner. Sweat slicked my palms as we strode toward the revolving door and safety. My stomach churned, over-wrought with anxiety. Two paces from the door, someone called my name. Sam had his phone to his ear, deep into a terse conversation with his assistant about a flight to Madrid, and proceeded out the door. I tried to avoid the voice, but a hand grabbed my elbow. I gasped and whirled around to find Jared smiling at me.

"Hey, girl," he said, lifting an eyebrow. "Easy now." He raised his palms to face outward. "I come in peace."

"Jared." I pressed a hand to my chest. "You scared me."

"I can see that." He smiled again, his easy demeanor diminishing my stress.

"I'm sorry, but I can't talk." I gestured helplessly toward Sam, standing next to his car, frowning through the glass door at me.

"It's okay. Not a problem." He smiled again and extended his right arm, an envelope in his hand. "This is for you."

"What?" I took the envelope and turned it over to find it blank and smooth on all sides.

He winked at me while backing away. "Just a little incentive from the boss man," he said. He pointed at me with thumb and forefinger. "Catch you later, babe."

Before I could say more, he disappeared into a flood of people exiting the bank of elevators. I shrugged and shoved the envelope into my purse, assuming it to be an invitation of some kind to one of his hedonistic parties.

Once inside the car, Sam ignored me, choosing instead to scroll through messages on his phone and conduct more business calls. I hugged the door, my attention focused on the passing scenery outside. After a few blocks, I remembered the envelope in my purse and retrieved it. Inside, I found a handwritten check for ten thousand dollars signed by Maxwell Seaforth, along with a small note that said, *Installment 1 of 5.* My stomach churned and for a brief moment, I thought I might be sick.

A quick glance at Sam showed him to be entranced in his conversation, oblivious to my impending meltdown. I shoved the note and check back into the envelope. Ten thousand dollars was a lot of money. I had to admit, for the briefest of seconds, I considered cashing it. Sam hated me. I was going to lose my job. Crockett was in jail. My mother was ill and needed my support. The money could go a long way in sustaining my family.

I immediately squashed the notion as soon as it surfaced. I'd already been down the path of temptation and knew it led nowhere. Money only lasted a brief time. Eventually it would be spent, and I'd be left with nothing but my self-loathing. I fought the urge to tear up the check and fling the bits out the window. If Sam hadn't been sitting beside me, I would've done it, but I didn't want him to know.

I cast a surreptitious glance at Sam's profile. Longing fired through my body. Why did he have to be so gorgeous?

Late afternoon sunlight silhouetted his long eyelashes, straight nose, and the curve of his lips. How he was still single after all these years baffled me. I was certain a hundred girls would give anything to be his wife. I'd had the privilege and sold it. Now, I'd give anything to have it back.

"What?" he asked, catching my stare.

I flushed and shook my head, turning away.

I'd assumed my absence from Sam's life would heal the rift between him and his father. Apparently, I'd been oh-so wrong. The knowledge left me curiously deflated. I'd accepted a bribe to save my brother and to give Sam the life he'd been born to live. Instead, my brother continued to be a loser of the worst kind, and Sam had struck out on his own, becoming a success in spite of me. I turned to face him, needing to know the truth.

"What did you do afterward?" I blurted.

"Excuse me?" He glanced up at me, brow furrowed over whatever he was looking at. "I came downstairs and got in the car, made a few calls."

"No. I mean after I left you." During our separation, I'd found any mention of him too painful and had exorcised him from my life, forbidding friends and family to speak of him. I'd erased all my memories of him. Until now. I studied his face, still handsome through his confusion. Had he walked away from his father, in spite of my efforts? "After the divorce. What did you do?"

"Does it matter?" The muscles of his throat worked, holding back an emotion his face refused to exhibit.

"It does. Yes. It matters. A lot." I dared to rest a hand on his knee. His gaze dropped to it before he blinked up to meet my eyes. A muscle in his jaw ticked.

"I fell apart for a while." His gaze held mine, vivid green and unforgiving. Pain and resentment roiled unfettered in the depths of his black pupils. This was my punishment. More punishment. Would it never end? "I was reckless. I went skydiving, bungee jumping, raced cars. I drank too much, did drugs, lived life on the edge." He glanced out the window as if remembering gutted him. "I fucked a hundred nameless girls, trying to erase your memory."

Even though his last confession gutted me, I pressed on, determined to hear the truth. "But you didn't go back to your father?"

He snorted. "Hell no. I went my own way. I had a trust fund from my mother that I got at twenty-five. I used it to buy out a friend's business. Started building on it." When his focus returned to me, it blazed with unnerving intensity. "I wanted to show you what you'd lost, that I could be successful on my own. To make you regret leaving me, for taking his money." His features hardened, chilling me. "I blame him for tempting you as much as I blame you for accepting the temptation."

The weight of his answer settled over me like a ten-ton shackle. My actions had spurred him into self-destruction. I'd ruined my beautiful boy. Tears blurred my eyes. "I'm so sorry," I whispered.

"Save it," he said, his tone cold and unforgiving. "Too little, too late, Dakota." The phone in his hand buzzed with an incoming call. He answered with a brusque, "Seaforth," and dismissed me without a second glance.

We didn't speak again, even when Rockwell dropped me at my apartment. It was early evening by this time. Sam didn't look up when I got out of the car, and I didn't look back.

31

DAKOTA - THEN

WHEN I heard the door to my apartment creak open, sweet adrenalin flooded my system. Quiet footsteps echoed through the long hall toward the kitchen where I stood over the stove, stirring a stock pot full of my mother's stew. The closer the steps grew, the faster the blood roared through my veins.

"Mmmmm. Smells good." Sam's deep, quiet voice purred into my ear. He wrapped his arms around my waist and pressed a kiss to the tender flesh at the pulse point beneath my jaw.

"Mom," I said with a laugh. "She thinks we're going to starve to death."

On our graduation night, Sam had proposed, and we'd gotten married at the county courthouse a week later. He'd placed a plain gold band on my ring finger, thin and inexpensive, but it meant the world to me. My mother had gone with us, the only witness to our marriage besides the handful of others in the courtroom.

Because Sam was now poor, we'd skipped the honeymoon, choosing instead to spend the time settling into our dingy, new basement apartment. He worked a full-time job at a construction company, installing roofs during the day, and went to college at night. I kept my part-time job at the convenience store and got another job cleaning hotel rooms in the morning before classes. It was tough living, but we were too young to know any better. Every minute spent with Sam made the struggle worth it.

By now, we'd been married almost two years, but the sight of him still made my heart kick against my ribs. I turned to face him and gave him a deep, lingering kiss. He pulled back and glanced longingly at the stew.

"I can't stay. I've got class in thirty minutes," he said.

"You can take it with you," I said, always eager to be a good wife. He shot me a slap on the ass and a lopsided grin then took a seat at the table. I cast a sideways glance at him while I dipped stew into a thermos. Exhaustion smudged beneath his eyes. He was thinner than I liked to see. His eyelids fluttered with exhaustion. Catching sight of my frown, he winked, and a bevy of butterflies unfurled in my stomach.

"Maybe you should skip class tonight," I said as I handed the Thermos to him. "We could watch a movie. Go to bed early."

"Can't," he replied and stood. "Got a midterm tonight."

"Right." I followed him to the door.

He bent and kissed me. "I want you naked and in my bed when I get home," he said. One of his hands patted my butt. "Understand, woman?"

"Anything you want, baby," I whispered and clung to his shirt, suddenly overcome with unreasonable fear. "I love you, Sam."

"Love you, too."

I watched him get in the car, a knot of dread tightening my gut. The knot remained as I put away the stew and wiped down the kitchen counter. When the doorbell rang, I flew to the door, thinking Sam had returned and forgotten his key. I flung open the door and came face to face with Mr. Seaforth.

"Hello, Dakota," he said. "Can I come in?"

I hesitated. I hadn't seen Mr. Seaforth since he'd confronted me at the convenience store two years earlier. Once Sam knew what he'd done, an irreparable rift had opened between father and son. To my knowledge, they hadn't seen or spoken to each other since.

"Sure." I pushed the door open and led him into the living room. His gaze roved over the shabby furniture with obvious distaste. A flush of embarrassment heated my cheeks. "Would you like some coffee or lemonade?"

"No. I'm fine." His frank stare raked over me.

"Sam just left for class. He'll be back later if you—"

"I'm here to see you, Dakota," he said. He shifted to the edge of the couch as if he might dirty his linen suit by lingering there. He opened his jacket and withdrew a white envelope. When he extended it to me, I took it out of instinct.

"What's this?" I turned the envelope over, confused.

"It's for you. A bank draft." The coldness in his expression sent a shiver of pure terror down my spine. "One million dollars."

The envelope burned my fingers like acid. I dropped it into his lap. "No. I can't take it. Sam wouldn't like it."

"That's why I'm here, Dakota. For Sam. He's not happy here." Once again, his eyes roved the apartment. I saw the place through his eyes, through Sam's eyes. Peeling wallpaper. Dirty carpet. A disgusting yellow stain of questionable origin on the ceiling.

"We're doing just fine." I stood, intending to shoo him out the door, but he placed a hand on my wrist and pulled me back down to the couch.

"You're not fine. Look at this place." His lips curled in a sneer. "Sam has always had the best of everything. You can't believe he wants this." I bit my lower lip, unsure of the best way to get this man out of my house. "He gave up everything for you, and this is how you repay him? By holding him back?" He shook his head. "I can still get him into Princeton. He can have the best the world has to offer. All you need to do is take the money, Dakota."

A wave of fury unlike any I'd ever known swept through me. I stood again. "You need to leave. In case you haven't noticed, Sam and I are married. Until death do us part."

He sighed, weary of the pretense of politeness. "Very well. I hoped you would make this easy but since you won't, here's the deal. Your brother, Crockett? He stole a few very valuable items from our house." As he spoke, he withdrew a second envelope and opened it to display a sheaf of documents, along with a DVD. He tapped the silver disc. "I have it all on video from our security cameras. There's enough evidence on there to put your brother away for quite a while, and I can make it happen."

Unmitigated terror churned the contents of my stomach. This couldn't be happening, could it? An hour ago, I'd been blissfully happy, secure in my marriage, with a husband who loved me. Now, my world had been upturned. I knew without doubt that my life was about to change forever.

"You can't do this," I whispered.

"I can, and I will." A satisfied smirk twisted his features. "Sign these divorce papers. Take the money. I'll make all of this go away like that." He snapped his fingers. "Or do nothing. Your brother will go to prison, and I'll fire your mother. I'll see that she never works again."

32

DAKOTA - NOW

ANOTHER WEEK passed. Sam drifted in and out of the office without speaking to me. He emailed a list of requests directly to my computer each day. No more fussy, detailed demands. Most of the tasks regarded scouting potential building sites for a series of residential subdivisions in central Illinois. This was my specialty, and something at which I excelled, but I missed the challenge of his silly lists and the thought he'd put into creating them.

Dahlia settled into my former office and hovered around the cubicles like a vulture circling dead meat. The sight of her smug face behind my burled walnut desk set my teeth on edge. Once an hour or so, she ventured out into the "general population," as Brian called it, to monitor company morale, which had hit an all-time low. An undercurrent of tension threaded throughout the floor, more reminiscent of a funeral parlor than the upbeat business it had been. Bit by bit, Sam was dismantling Harmony.

I ate lunch at my desk, a pathetic meal of crackers and

cheese, while organizing my research for Sam. Stress had killed my appetite, and I'd lost almost ten pounds since the takeover.

The list of properties Sam had given me was standard fare. Most of them were farmland. A few were lower-income subdivisions. I gathered information regarding pricing, availability, and asked Melody to obtain demographics for the area. All the locations had stellar growth potential, and I was impressed with his choices, except for the last two places. I hadn't heard of them before and they seemed unrelated to anything we'd discussed in our meetings. These remote parcels of land outside of Gary, Indiana, seemed completely inappropriate in both location and potential.

Why would he even bother with such inferior prospects? At first I thought it might have been a mistake, or perhaps he'd given me the wrong information. I toyed with the idea of calling him to clarify the address but hesitated. We hadn't had an actual conversation since our meeting on Monday. He haunted my every waking thought and all of my dreams. I craved his touch, his approval, one word or gesture that might suggest there was a chance for us. My thumb hovered over Sam's name in my contact list as I debated whether or not to dial. Before I could come to a decision, the phone vibrated with an incoming call, the number unfamiliar. I tapped a finger on the desk in contemplation then answered it.

"Dakota Atwell."

"Ms. Atwell." The voice on the other end of the call sent dread straight into my gut. "This is Maxwell Seaforth."

"I know who it is," I said and hung up. Screw the bastard. It rang again immediately. I sighed, knowing he wouldn't give up until I answered. After darting a glance around the deserted office, I accepted the call and said, "What do you want?"

"You haven't cashed my check yet. I've got another ready and waiting. What's the holdup?" His smooth voice conjured visions of the fiery pits of hell, which was exactly where any association with this man would lead me.

"No, and I'm not going to. Don't call me again." I disconnected the call. Tremors shook my entire body. I threw the phone across the desk and clasped my hands together until my knuckles ached.

The man had some nerve. Why did he continue to haunt me? Was I such a threat to his empire? I was nothing, nobody. An ache bloomed between my temples. I rubbed the space between my brows to ease the tension. Sam had made a success of his life in spite of his father's efforts to control him. That was what it was about for Maxwell Seaforth. Control. I sat up a little straighter in my chair. He'd never been able to control Sam. Sam had always done what he wanted, whether his father liked it or not, until I came along. He'd used me to manipulate Sam, and I'd fallen right into his plans. Neither of us could have predicted that Sam was too strong and too pigheaded to submit.

"Dakota? Can I see you in my office, please?" Dahlia's voice cut into my thoughts. She had sidled up to me, stealthy like a damned ninja.

I followed her through the maze of cubicles to her office, the one I'd so lovingly decorated, and tried not to dwell on the pettiness of ownership or material things. She offered a seat in the chair across from the desk. We stared at each other for an interminable beat. I'd never been on the other side of my desk, and I didn't like it.

"How are you doing since the acquisition?" she asked,

folding her hands on the desk between us. Sunlight cut through the windows behind her, turning her gold hair to silver. "Are you making the adjustment okay?"

"Yes." I leaned back and crossed my legs. Her patronizing tone ruffled my composure. "Is there some concern about my performance?"

"You're on probation," she said. "I'm sure it must be uncomfortable for you, knowing you might get the ax at any time." The smug smirk on her over-glossed lips caused my fingers to tighten into fists. The weight of uncertainty settled back around my shoulders. "Mr. Seaforth asked me to check on you, to make sure you're adhering to our company guidelines. He's very concerned you won't make the second cut."

All of my insecurities rallied and steamrolled over my fragile self-confidence. Sam had discussed me with Dahlia? Although we'd been at odds for most of the past month, his small sporadic kindnesses and our lovemaking had given me a glimmer of hope. "If he has any issues with my performance, he hasn't said anything. Quite the contrary, actually." I decided to bluff my way through the conversation.

A glimmer of panic sparked in her eyes. "Really?" She reclined in her chair, which I knew from experience was much more comfortable than the rigid one I sat in, and studied my face. "He hadn't mentioned it to me. Of course, we'll be having dinner tonight. I'll be sure to ask him about it."

Suddenly, I felt like a fool. Jealousy, bitter and cold, left a bad taste in my mouth. I stood and gave her a tight smile. "Is there anything else? I need to make a few more calls before I leave today."

"No. That's it. Thank you, Dakota."

I gave her a cool nod and walked out the door. The constant uncertainties and insecurities of the past ten years had been exhausting. I needed to put an end to the madness I'd created. A sense of calm washed over me. I knew what I needed to do. The time had come to make things right.

The next day, I arrived at work an hour early with a renewed sense of determination. Sam arrived a few minutes after me, went straight into his office, and closed the door with a bang. I jumped, my nerves already atwitter at the thought of what I was about to do. I waited ten long tense minutes, giving him time to settle in, before knocking on his door.

"What is it?" he asked. Judging by the dark shadows smudged beneath his eyes, he hadn't been sleeping well either.

"Do you have a minute?" I asked, a flutter of nerves bouncing around in my stomach.

"No." He passed a hand over his face then reconsidered. "Fine. Five minutes."

I placed the brown cardboard folder on his desk and smoothed a hand over the surface. It felt cold and solid under my hand, but inside it possessed all the secrets to my past. His brows drew together. "It's all in here," I said, tapping the folder. "All of it. The contract, a copy of the check." I drew the envelope from my pocket, the one Jared had given to me. "And his latest attempt to bribe me."

"I don't understand." Sam leaned back in his chair, studying me.

"You will," I said. As my final gesture, I laid the USB drive containing a copy of his father's threats on top of the brown folder, along with my letter of resignation. I turned to leave.

"Wait," he said when my hand touched the door handle. For the first time in a decade, a ray of hope broke through the gray clouds of my life.

The longer Sam listened to the recording of my conversation with his father, the redder his face became. A storm swirled through his vibrant irises. Once the recording stopped, he turned his chair toward the wall of windows behind his desk and sat in silence. Dread churned in my stomach. Knowing he couldn't possibly hate me more than he already did, I decided to plunge headlong into the abyss of self-destruction.

"I know what you must be thinking," I began, struggling to hide the tremulous waver in my voice. I braced to receive his derision.

He stood from his chair and walked to the far end of the office, gazing down on the street below. "You have no idea what I'm thinking." The disdain in his tone killed the vestiges of my control. Over the course of my career, I'd been dressed down by intimidating men and had stood my ground without flinching, but the reality of facing Sam's wrath terrified me more than anything. I began to shake from head to toe until my knees dissolved into water. I sank into the chair by the door and waited.

"If you want me to go, I'll understand," I said the second I found my voice again. It floated in the space between us, detached and foreign to my ears. "You've got my resignation. It nullifies the contract."

"Maybe it's for the best," he replied.

Unshed tears of defeat stung my eyelids. Karma was a

cold-hearted bitch, and she'd stolen around to bite me in the ass. I stood to leave for the final time. Maybe I was defeated and maybe I deserved his hatred, but I took comfort in knowing I'd done the right thing at last. Sam's father would never again use me as a pawn in his sick mind games.

With my eyes down, I trudged to my desk and began to gather the few belongings I kept there. A picture of my mother, another of Crockett, a few cosmetic items, and my purse. I'd dedicated everything I had to this job, and all I had to show for it was a box full of trinkets. Curious eyes watched from afar, but no one ventured to my side. I felt a pang of empathy for Muriel.

By the time I'd put the final items into the box, I heard Sam's door open. The prickling of the tiny hairs on my arms told me he was nearby. He laid an envelope on top of the box in my arms.

"It's your severance check," he said. A muscle ticked in his jaw. "Two weeks. I think it's more than reasonable under the circumstances."

Although the envelope contained a mere slip of paper, it felt like a two-ton weight in my arms. I set the box on the desk, took the envelope, and without opening it, ripped it in half. Sam stared at me, disbelief and confusion clouding his eyes.

"I don't want your money, Sam," I said, in a clear, strong voice. "It was never about the money then, and it's not about the money now."

With my head held high and my box of belongings, I made the long trek through the cubicles. No one spoke as I passed. The elevator car arrived after what felt like hours. The bell dinged, and the doors slid open with a quiet *shoosh*. When I turned around, I saw Sam still standing at my desk, his blond head and shoulders visible above the cubicle dividers. Our eyes met. I gave him a small smile even though my insides ached. I'd probably never see him again, but I felt a heavy load had lifted from my shoulders. For the first time in a long time, I was proud of myself, and it felt better than a million dollars in the bank.

33

DAKOTA - NOW

WHEN I passed through the revolving doors, I saw Rockwell waiting at the curb, leaning against the fender of the BMW. I gave him a small smile. To my surprise, he met me on the sidewalk and took the box from my arms.

"Mr. Seaforth asked me to drive you home," he said. His voice gave nothing away.

I tried to take the box back, but he lifted a warning eyebrow. "Are you sure about that?"

"Absolutely," he replied.

We stood on the sidewalk at an impasse, both of us clinging to the box.

"I'd rather walk," I said and gave the box a stubborn tug.

He smiled at me over the contents but didn't let go. "I understand." His eyes met mine without judgment or guile. "Go ahead and walk, miss. I'll follow along with your belongings."

An image of Rockwell in the limousine, trailing a teenaged Sam and me as we walked after school, brought the sting of tears to my eyes. I released the box and fought back a torrent of emotion. My lower lip quivered. I felt ridiculous and young, heartbroken and euphoric, all at the same time.

"Okay," I said, suddenly overcome by the impact of what I'd done. By giving Sam that folder, I'd put an end to a decade of secrets, as well as my career and any hopes of a reconciliation. The enormity of that one simple act rippled through me like a stone thrown into water. It was over. I was free. So why did I feel so miserable?

Rockwell placed the box in the trunk of the car, while I stood on the sidewalk and watched, numb and disconnected. He gripped my arm above the elbow with a gloved hand and guided me gently into the back seat. The door closed behind me, muting the sounds of traffic and construction. Soft notes of classical music drifted in the cool quiet of the car's interior. Rockwell cast a concerned glance into the rearview mirror before easing the car into the avenue.

My insides ached, collapsing on the emptiness within me. The thought of sitting in my empty apartment during a Monday filled me with panic. I had no direction, no purpose. I'd never taken a vacation day or called in sick. I had no idea how to do anything but work.

"Rockwell?"

"Miss?"

"Can you take me somewhere else, please?" I gave him the new address. He listened then nodded and changed our route without question.

I stared out the window. Bright June sunshine spilled onto the streets and houses. I watched people and cars flash by in a blur. Each person had his or her own story. I wondered how many of them were like me, sorting out their mistakes, swayed by temptation and dealing with the consequences of poor choices.

"I never stopped loving him," I said aloud.

"I'm sorry, miss?" Rockwell said. His gaze flicked to mine in the rearview mirror.

"Sam. I never left him because I didn't love him," I said, bursting with the need to tell someone who understood the situation. "I've hated myself every day since then. I just wanted to save Crockett from going to jail. He was so young, only fourteen. And Mr. Seaforth said he'd fire my mother. He said Sam was better off without me, that I was keeping him from living the life he deserved." I bit my lower lip to stop the torrent of confessions. Heat rushed into my cheeks. I turned back to the window, embarrassed at the outburst.

A full five minutes passed before Rockwell replied. "It nearly broke him when you left. He came to me. Stayed with me for a month or so until he got back on his feet. He didn't know about his father's part in everything. Mr. Seaforth said you asked for the money, but I don't think Sam ever believed it." He paused at an intersection and waited until the light changed before he continued. "I don't know if it makes a difference or not, but there was never anyone else. Sure, there were girls—he's a handsome boy— but he never got serious with any of them. I knew the first time we took you home in the limo that he was a goner. And if you ask me, miss, nothing's changed."

We found my mother working in the yard outside her front door. She wore a loose blue dress, a print apron tied around her waist. At her feet, a vibrant mix of purple pansies, red tulips, and yellow dahlias burst from an oval flowerbed. She straightened at the sight of the unfamiliar car and flattened a hand over her eyes to cut the glare of the noonday sun.

Rockwell had barely brought the vehicle to a stop when I flung open the door and charged at her. She caught me in her arms, nestling my head to the crook of her neck, and squeezed me.

"Baby? What's wrong? Is Crockett okay?" She loosened her hold and leaned back far enough to see my face.

"He's fine," I said.

One of her hands stroked my hair, soothing my angst. "Then what is it?" At the concern in her voice, I felt foolish and pushed away from her. "Are you ill?"

"I'm sorry. I'm fine. I didn't mean to worry you." I searched her gaze, finding comfort in the quiet calm of her blue-green eyes. "I just needed you."

Warmth diminished the lines of age on her face. "A mother always likes to hear that," she said. Her agile fingers untied the apron around her waist.

"Oh, Mom," I said, overcome with relief. The words tumbled out of me like water from a pitcher. "I told Sam everything about his dad and the money and Crockett. And then I quit. I'm sure he really hates me now. He'll never forgive me." I paused to check for her reaction. "I still love him, Mom."

"Well, I can hardly wait to hear the details." She put an arm around my shoulders to usher me toward the house. "Come on inside. I'll fix some tea. You can tell me all about it."

Rockwell coughed. I'd forgotten about him again. We both turned to face him. Joy brightened my mother's smile. "Rockwell? Oh my goodness. How long has it been?"

"Ten years, give or take a month or two," he said. His eyes twinkled. "But you don't look a day older."

"You sly fox," she said, blushing, and swatted him with her apron. "Won't you come inside? I'd love to catch up."

"I don't think so," he said, shifting his gaze to mine. "I wouldn't want to intrude. Maybe another time?"

"Nonsense," Mom said. She grabbed his arm and tugged him toward the front door. "I've got fresh apple pie and ice cream."

"Homemade?" he asked.

"Would I have any other kind?"

We sat around the kitchen table eating pie while I spilled the entire story to my mother. Well, my mother and Rockwell ate. I just pushed the food around my dish, having lost my appetite. Mother nodded in understanding, adding an occasional exclamation or patting my hand now and then when my voice cracked. Rockwell concentrated on his pie and ate two helpings, to my mother's great excitement.

Exhausted by the events of the day, I collapsed in a boneless puddle on the living room sofa. Rockwell and my mother stayed in the kitchen, talking and laughing over coffee. I found their voices comforting, a reminder of the past, and let myself drift into sleep. Tomorrow, I would make a plan. Somehow, I'd get through this, even if it killed me.

34

SAMUEL - NOW

LATER IN the day, Rockwell met me at the curb in front of the building. The cool interior of the car cocooned around me like a protective haven. Once inside, I withdrew the brown folder from my briefcase and stared at it. I scarcely knew what to make of the contents. For the third time, I read the contract. In very specific terms, it forbade Dakota from ever contacting me or my family, offered absolution to Crockett, and promised employment to her mother for the duration of her life. A DVD showed Crockett in action, committing a variety of crimes including the theft of several valuable pieces of jewelry from my mother's bedroom.

I ruffled my hair, overcome with rage so violent, I felt the need to smash something. My father had blackmailed her into leaving me. Now, he was at it again. The recording from her phone and the uncashed check proved his nefarious plans.

By the time we arrived at Seaforth Towers, my anger had receded to an even simmer. I needed to keep my wits about me. Although I'd been to the Towers on business numerous times, I'd never once seen my father.

The lady at the lobby reception desk seemed nonplussed by my appearance. She rang his office and after a few tense moments, nodded toward the bank of elevators. "He said to come right up. He's been expecting you."

The elevator ride took forever, but it gave me time to pull myself together. When I stepped off the elevator, a flurry of whispers and stares whirled around the office. The décor was gray granite and shiny chrome, devoid of warmth or welcome, just like my father. A svelte blonde in an immaculate black pantsuit escorted me down the long hallway to his office.

He was standing in front of an impressive wall of windows, all the better to survey his kingdom, I supposed, and turned to greet me upon my entrance. We stared at each other, together for the first time in years. He looked the same but older, his face more lined, his hair more silver, and his back a bit more stooped. I ignored his proffered hand and swept my gaze over the plush black carpet, the framed original prints on the walls, and the decadent modern furniture.

"It's great to see you, Samuel," he said, recovering from my snub and returning to sit behind his massive desk. "Have a seat. Would you like a drink? Bourbon?"

"This isn't a social call," I said and plopped the brown folder on his desk before easing into the chair across from him.

"Gosh, it's been a while, hasn't it?" he said, a genuine smile on his face. "You look good."

"Cut the bullshit." His easy demeanor pissed me off. How could he act so cavalier when he'd been so detrimental to my life? He'd stolen the one thing I'd ever cared about—Dakota. How could a father treat his son with such disregard? "I'm just here to tell you, I know everything."

He lifted an eyebrow. "About what?"

"About Dakota. The way you coerced her. The way you're trying to bribe her now." A muscle in his jaw ticked, but his eyes remained bright.

"Look, I don't know what she's told you, but you can't believe a word she says." He leaned forward on an elbow. "The girl's a money whore, for goodness sake. She'll do just about anything for the right price."

I thought about Dakota's modest apartment and the way she'd torn up my severance check. Nothing could be further from the truth. His words raised the hackles on my neck. I narrowed my eyes. "This folder contains the original contract, the DVD of Crockett with Mom's jewels, a recording of your encounter with Dakota in the elevator, and the check Jared gave her." The color in his face faded. He swallowed hard. "You make me sick." I stood and turned to leave.

"Now, Samuel. Be reasonable." He moved toward the door with me, stepping in front of it to block my way. "I'm only trying to protect you from yourself. She's not worth it. I can't believe you'd be so stupid as to fall for her tricks again."

I squared my shoulders. "The only person I need protection from is you. Stay out of my life. It's the last time I'm going to say it."

"Wait." He placed a hand on my shoulder. At the sight of my expression, he dropped his hand. "I just want you to come back. I need you here at Seaforth Towers. I'm not getting any younger. Someday this will all be yours." He made a passive gesture to encompass the room.

"You just don't get it," I said. "I don't need you or your money. I don't want all this."

Temper flared in his eyes. "What you need is a good, stiff reality check," he snapped. "Wake up, Sam. Like it or not, you're a Seaforth." I stepped back a pace, as if he'd punched me. "Oh, I've followed your career quite closely. You've done me proud. I've watched you rip business after business apart, devour them, and spit out the bones. You hate me, but you've become just like me."

A knot began to tighten in my gut. "You're wrong. I'm nothing like you," I said, but my confidence wavered.

"No, Sam. You're exactly like me, and I've got MacGruder to prove it. I led you to him, knowing you'd be able to acquire him when I couldn't. You took the bait and swallowed it, hook, line, and sinker." His smug smirk made me sick. "All we need to do is merge our two companies, and we'll have the market cornered."

"Seaforth and Son?" I quirked an eyebrow, recovering my composure.

"If you like," he said. "I was thinking more like Seaforth and Seaforth, but whatever."

"The deal isn't done. What if I back out?"

"You won't. You can't. If you don't go through with this, it'll put a stain on your reputation," he said. "People will say you're losing your edge. They won't be afraid of you anymore. Fear is a powerful motivator—just ask Dakota."

My fist curled with the urge to punch him. I closed my eyes and tried to think of one reason to resist. A picture of Dakota's face floated over my closed eyelids. I hated him for what he'd done to her, to us, and I hated myself for letting it change me into someone I no longer respected. My resolve bolstered, I met his eyes.

"We're done here," I said, in a cold, flat tone.

"You'll be back." He laughed as I brushed past him. "You can't deny who you are or what you've become. It's in your blood."

"We'll see about that," I muttered and let the door close behind me.

35

DAKOTA - NOW

A N ENTIRE week passed. As if things weren't bad enough, a zit erupted on my forehead, right between my eyes, larger than Mount Vesuvius and ready to blow. I covered it with pimple cream and resolved to stay hidden until it receded. I spent the time sleeping and eating all the food my mother had insisted on sending home with me.

Part of me knew I should get up and get cracking to find another job. I had friends and contacts. Maybe MacGruder would have a lead for me. Before I could even consider seeking employment, I needed to get myself together. I was still too raw and broken up about Sam to put a coherent sentence together, let alone sit for a job interview.

The following week, an insistent banging woke me from fitful dreams peppered with Sam's face. I glanced around my bedroom, disoriented. Previous events rushed back and smacked me on the head. Oh, yes. I was divorced, unemployable, and broke. I rubbed the sleep from my eyes. The banging resumed.

"Okay. I'm coming. Geez." Furious at the unscheduled

interruption of my misery, I searched for my robe. The apartment was in shambles. I hadn't done laundry in weeks. With a sigh, I snatched a trench coat from the closet and stomped through the living room, shoving my arms through the sleeves like a fretful maniac. "Do you have any idea what time it is?"

I lifted on tiptoe to peer through the peephole. A green eye stared back at me. *Oh, my.* My heart skittered and skipped. Sam? I peeked again. He stepped back a pace and frowned at the door. His hair was ruffled like he'd just run a hand through it.

"Dakota?" The sound of his mellow voice melted my knees and liquefied my bones. He knocked again.

"Um, just a minute," I called in my most pleasant voice then spun in a panicked circle. I ran my fingers through my hair. A glance in the mirror by the door showed a face devoid of makeup and the horrifying red zit between my brows. Sam knocked again. I grabbed a knit cap from the coat rack and crammed it on my head, pulling it low over my forehead to cover the offending pimple, then sniffed my armpits. At least I'd showered before bed and smelled clean.

"Dakota? I don't have all day," Sam said.

I opened the door. He jumped, one fist poised in the air, about to knock once more. His gaze travelled over me. I was wearing an old T-shirt and tiny shorts of mismatched colors beneath my coat. One eyebrow lifted as his focus returned to my face and the hat on my head.

"Am I interrupting something?" he asked.

"No. I was still in bed." Blood thundered so loudly in my veins, I could barely hear. The sight of him standing in my apartment unfurled a bevy of butterflies in my tummy. He was wearing a charcoal suit. His crisp white shirt was unbuttoned at the collar. The tail of his necktie dangled from his breast pocket. "What are you doing here?"

"Can I come in?"

I stepped back in equal measures of trepidation and excitement. I realized too late there were piles of dirty clothes on the sofa, empty pizza boxes and candy bar wrappers littering the counters and coffee table. I wrapped my arms around my waist, pulling the coat tighter, and tried to look casual while every nerve in my body danced. "Did you need something?"

"I just wanted to talk to you for a minute." He shoved a hand through his hair and frowned. "Did you have a party here or something?"

"No. I've just been busy and things." I spied a pair of panties on the end table and stuffed them into my pocket. "What did you want to talk about?"

Suddenly the air between us shifted. The scent of his cologne drifted over to me. I drew in a heady lungful. I leaned toward him, drawn to him, the way I'd always been. With his tousled hair and his hands in his pockets, he looked like the Sam I'd married. It took all of my control to keep from launching myself into his arms. A dull ache spread through my chest, knowing I'd never have him again.

"Look," he said. "I might've been a bit hasty in accepting your resignation." My mouth fell open in shock. He raised a hand. "The MacGruder deal isn't done yet, and I'd feel a lot better if you were around to help me close the deal."

"You want me back?" I asked, unable to believe his words. "Are you sure?"

He shrugged and blinked away. The muscles in his throat worked when he swallowed. When he looked back to me, his eyes were vibrant and alive. My pulse accelerated, and a rush of need poured through me.

"You can come back as a consultant," he said. "Same salary. Just until the deal's done."

My toes curled with the urge to do a happy dance. I smoothed my hands over my coat and tried to be cool. "I don't know. I'm pretty busy these days," I said, sweeping an arm around the apartment.

"Why are you wearing a winter coat and hat?" he asked suddenly. "It's eighty degrees outside." One corner of his lips twitched. I smiled, a wave of shyness bringing heat into my cheeks. He shook his head. "Get dressed. I'll send Rockwell back to get you in an hour."

36

DAKOTA - NOW

FTER A hasty shower, I tried on a dozen outfits before finally choosing a tailored black suit. The short skirt and jacket suggested sophistication with a bit of sass. I pinned my hair into a twist at the nape of my neck, letting the ends trail in spirals over one shoulder, and arranged the bangs to cover the ugly zit. In the elevator, I tapped a quick text to my mother about the unexpected turn in events, and she responded with, *Go get 'em, girl.* Rockwell met me at the curb next to a new car, a sleek white limousine. He smiled and nodded as he opened the door for me.

"Good morning, miss," he said.

"Hi, Rockwell." I cast a warm smile in his direction. "My mom said to tell you hello."

"I trust she's well?"

"Yes." The smile slipped from my face when I spied a long leg clad in black trousers inside the car. My gaze travelled up the leg and found it attached to Sam. One of his big hands curled around his cellphone. He glanced up as I slid into the car and gave me a tentative smile.

"Good morning," he said.

"Hi." The greeting came out squeaky and girlish. I swallowed and tried to appear calm, despite the spike of adrenalin running through me at the sight of him. "I didn't expect to see you."

He cocked an eyebrow. "You were expecting someone else?" He tucked the phone into the inside pocket of his jacket and ran his gaze over me. I warmed under his perusal. By the gleam in his eyes, he approved of the dress.

"No, I just thought you were busy."

Rockwell shut the door behind me, enveloping us in a private cocoon of automotive splendor. The car pulled smoothly away from the apartment complex. Outside the tinted windows, the sunlight of the city sparkled over the building windows like gemstones. Sam leaned forward and handed me a bottle of my favorite flavored sparkling water. The tips of his fingers brushed my knuckles. Heat and desire mingled in our touch.

"I don't understand." I took a sip of the water, parched. It tickled over my tongue in a dance of bubbles and sweetness. "Aren't we going back to the office?"

"Yes. To my office." He lifted his water bottle and took a drink. When he swallowed, the motion of his throat muscles mesmerized me. The way his tongue swept over his lower lip. The drift of his gaze over my face, along the curves of my breasts, the stretch of my legs, and back to my mouth. A sweet pang of desire buzzed through me.

"What's Dahlia going to say about this?" I asked, peering at him over the top of my water.

He shrugged. "It's none of her business."

"Are you two an item?" I asked.

"We were never an item," he replied. His gaze lingered

on my lips, the same way it had the very first time he'd taken me home in his limo after school.

"It's bad form to sleep with your employees," I chastised.

He spread his knees wider until one of them grazed my leg. His hands rested on top of his thighs while his eyes continued to watch me with unnerving intensity. I took another sip of water, hoping to calm my nerves.

"I never sleep with my employees, although I have fucked a few." When he shifted in the seat, the delicious friction of his pant leg against my knee sent a shockwave of desire along my limbs.

"Do you still want to fuck me?" I couldn't tear my eyes away from his. They glowed in the ambient light of the car's interior, like green molten lava.

"I never stopped," he said. The quiet husk of his voice elicited dampness between my legs. I licked my lips. One of his hands left his leg to finger the hem of my skirt. A frisson of excitement blossomed in my belly and migrated south to my core. "This looks good on you."

I'd worn sheer black stockings held up by a red garter belt to match my red panties and bra. I uncrossed my legs, feeling the slide and glide of silk against my skin. His fingers brushed over my knee as I turned toward him.

"Do you hate me?" My breath hitched as his hand travelled beneath the dress, climbing higher along the inside of my thigh, and came to a stop at the lace trim of my panties.

"Never." One of his fingers traced the edge. I opened my legs to allow his hand access. His gaze remained locked with mine. The span of his chest rose and fell with a heavy sigh.

"I thought I wasn't worth it," I whispered on a ragged exhale.

He dragged a finger along my folds, testing the wetness. Need began to coil tightly inside me. "I only said it to break you." His voice rumbled in his chest, deep and rasping. My gaze flew to his, finding his eyes fiery and darkening by the second. "I didn't realize you were already broken."

He leaned forward, gliding his other hand up my leg to curl around my hip. He pulled me to his lap, arranging my knees alongside the outside of his thighs. Each of his movements was slow, measured and deliberate. As if he might spook me by moving too fast. As if it took all of his control to keep from throwing me to the seat and pounding the hell out of me.

I looked into his eyes, needing reassurance, and found a cautious vulnerability that squeezed my heart. Deep inside this beautiful, angry man resided the boy I'd loved. The boy I'd hurt. The love of my life. The need to heal his wounds, to repair the damage I'd done, swept through me like an updraft of spring wind. I smoothed a hand through his hair, pushing it back from his face, and leaned forward to place a chaste kiss on the corner of his mouth. He made a strangled noise deep in his chest and closed his eyes, shutting me out. When they opened again, the pain and longing inside them ripped me open.

All at once, his control snapped. He fisted a hand in my hair and yanked my mouth to his. His tongue swept along mine, ravishing me from the inside out. I moaned and dug my fingers into his scalp. He jerked the hairpins from my updo, and the unruly locks tumbled over my shoulders. His grip on my hair tightened to the point of pain. He pulled my head back, exposing my neck like a vampire seeking blood. When his lips touched the tender flesh beneath my chin, they burned my skin with their heat.

He lifted his head, eyes blazing, and stared me down.

Any illusions I'd had about my sweet college boy vanished. Samuel was a man, and I had a feeling he was about to show me how much of a man he'd become. He continued to pull my head back. The flare of his nostrils as he took in my scent filled me with primal fear and longing.

"Never again," he rasped, in a voice so layered with emotion, it tore at my reserve. "You will never fuck me over again. Do you understand?"

"Yes," I whispered through the thickness of my throat. It was only one word, but it held a million different meanings for me. Yes, I loved him. Yes, I needed him. And yes, I understood better than he could ever know.

"Say it," he growled.

"Never again." I slipped my hand between us and palmed the hardness behind his zipper. My chest ached with longing and filled with his pain.

His fingers twisted in the delicate side-straps of my panties and with one hard jerk, tore them off. I ground against his erection then leaned back to undo the fly of his pants. He drew a condom from his pocket and once it was on, returned his lips to mine.

We kissed, long and hard, until my lips ached. He gripped my hips and thrust into me. I cried out, overwhelmed by the sweet familiarity of having him inside me. His big hands held me down while he impaled me. Our ragged respirations filled the quiet interior of the car and fogged the windows. He raged against me, jerking his hips upward with rapid, deep grunts. I let him take his revenge on my body while I worshipped him with lips and hands. I gave him everything I had, letting him drain me of the last vestiges of denial. I still loved him. I had always loved him and always would.

"Sam," I whispered into his neck, almost in tears. "My Sam."

"Your Sam," he said while his fingers made quick work of the buttons on my blouse.

With those words, I broke into a thousand pieces. I peppered kisses over his forehead, his nose, his eyelids, and his cheeks. His hands gripped my ass, rocking me into him. I leaned back, and his mouth found my breast. The sting of his teeth brought my nipple to a tight peak. A startled squeak hissed out of me. The shift in position put his cock in the secret spot inside me, the one where furious pleasure blended with sweet pain.

His hand found my throat. He stroked the column of my neck, murmuring nonsense, his lips burning my skin. I'd never wanted to please a man so much. I ran my hands over every inch of him, desperate to wipe away the pain of our separation, the bitterness of our divorce, and the sting of my betrayal. If only I could make him see how much I cared.

I cupped his face between my palms and stared into his eyes, willing him to understand. Our past flashed between us, building a bridge where none had existed. I saw his sweet smile the first time he'd kissed me, the glow in his eyes when he'd married me, and the heat of his passion on our wedding night. It was all still there, buried deep, but existent. I lifted and sank down on him, unable to control the wild swivel of my hips.

He came hard, face buried in the curve of my neck, his hands on my ass and his chest heaving. I followed a heartbeat later, my walls clutching and spasming around him, the sting of tears in my eyes, just as the car made the final turn to his office. With surprising presence of mind, he disentangled a hand from my ass and pressed the intercom to speak with Rockwell.

"Take us around the block once, would you?" he asked, his voice broken and shaking.

"Certainly," Rockwell replied, his voice disembodied through the speaker.

A sudden flood of uncertainty tightened my chest. What was I doing? Screwing my ex-husband, let alone my current boss, wasn't the brightest thing I'd ever done in life, and I'd done lots of stupid things.

Sam placed a finger beneath my chin and lifted my face to meet his gaze. Calm reassurance stared back at me. "Don't get all freaked out on me," he said. "I can see it in your eyes. You're working up to a meltdown, and I need you focused."

Seriously? The man had just fucked me senseless, and he expected me to focus? He was still inside me. The connection of our bodies superseded my panic, and I forced myself to relax.

"Right." I disentangled from him and returned to my seat. He disposed of the condom and adjusted his clothing, while I tried to reclaim some semblance of normalcy. My hair, frazzled by his fingers, seemed beyond repair. I did the best I could to capture the unruly locks with the few hair-pins I could find.

Sam watched me, expressionless, the picture of uncon-cern. Ten minutes earlier, he'd been trembling and passion-ate. His sudden apathy infuriated me. How could he make love to me then sit there, unmoving as granite, as if it didn't matter? My temper swelled until the blood pounded in my temples.

"So is this how it's going to be?" I asked. "Hot and cold? You fuck me and then you hate me? You fire me and then you hire me back?"

He stared out the window, a muscle ticking in his jaw. It

wasn't until Rockwell pulled in front of the building that he spoke. "I'm so goddam furious with you," he said at last, his voice a rough growl. "You should've come to me."

"I'm sorry?" I lifted an eyebrow, certain he'd gone off the deep end. The emotional rollercoaster ride of the past month had left me too exhausted to fight with him.

"All those years ago. When he blackmailed you. You should've told me." He turned the full force of his enigmatic eyes on me. They drilled into me with uncanny precision, hitting all the tender places inside me. "I would've protected you, Kota. We would've worked it out."

His use of my nickname scraped away the last of my defenses. I dropped my chin and stared at my hands in my lap, clenching and unclenching my fingers. "He had it all on video. Crockett stealing your stuff. Jewelry, prescriptions, money. It was over two hundred thousand dollars in total. He would've gone to prison for a very long time. He was only fourteen, Sam. Just a kid. And he said he'd fire my mother. I knew she wasn't well. She needed surgery. Thousands of dollars worth."

"Where is Crockett now?" Sam's voice whispered across the car, soft but edged with steel.

"He's in jail. I told him I won't bail him out of this one. He just keeps making the same mistakes over and over again. *I* keep making the same mistakes. We're alike in that way." I lifted my gaze to his and watched him through a blur of tears. "I only took the money to keep Crockett out of jail. To help my mom. He said you weren't happy with me, that you'd never be happy, and I believed him. I never wanted to hurt you. I loved you, Sam."

He curled his fingers around mine and lifted my hand to his lips to place a kiss on the back. We sat there for a very long time, staring at each other, remembering and regretting.

"I can't do this anymore," he said and let go of my hand. He opened the car door, and I followed him out. Disenchantment weighted my body. I knew the time had come for me to pay the final installment price. The devil was going to collect his due. I choked back the tears and steeled myself to accept whatever fate threw at me.

Rockwell tipped his hat at me. I gave him a brittle smile before looking up at Sam. He looked as unmovable as a marble statue with his square jaw clenched and his eyes narrowed.

"I can't do this anymore either." I clutched my purse and stared at him, wondering how we'd ever manage to get through the rest of the day together, let alone through the MacGruder deal. "Maybe it's better if we stopped torturing each other."

He passed a hand over his face and let out a groan of pure frustration. "Am I so bad at communicating?" he asked. "I meant I can't keep trying to hate you when I don't." A deep sigh deflated his chest. "Look. I'm not making any promises, but I'm willing to try this again if you are."

A wave of hope buoyed my weary soul. I dared to glance at his face and found nothing but sincerity in his expression. "I'd like that. But how can you ever trust me?"

"I don't know if I can." He shrugged, but some of the old light brightened his gaze. The corner of his mouth lifted in one of those rare smiles I'd come to cherish. He straightened the collar of his suit and tugged down the cuffs of his shirt. "We'll just have to see, I guess." With a touch soft as a whisper, he stroked the backs of his fingers along my jaw. "Okay with you, sweet pea?"

"Okay," I said. A brand-new kind of excitement tingled from my jaw down to my toes. I squinted up at him, his blond hair shining like a halo in the sunlight, eyes blazing down at me. Opportunity swirled around us. I pressed a hand to my stomach, awed by the way life could change in a heartbeat. Yesterday, I'd been drowning in defeat. Today, my future blossomed with possibilities.

I never knew how much Sam meant to me until I'd lost him. I never knew how much I wanted him until I couldn't have him. The chance to earn his forgiveness meant more than anything to me. If I'd learned anything from my mistakes, it was this. Love was priceless, especially when the one you loved loved you back.

Thank you for reading Foolish Mistakes, Book 1 of the Seaforth Billionaire Series. You can get more about Sam and Dakota's story in FOOLISH DECEPTION. Available now.

FELONY ROMANCE SERIES

Intoxicated

Unexpected

Vindicated

Impulsive

Drift

Committed

BAD BEHAVIOR SERIES

Bad Behavior #1

Bad Behavior #2

Bad Behavior #3

STANDALONES

Lies We Tell

SHORT STORIES

Everything

Linger

ABOUT THE AUTHOR

Jeana is a *USA Today* and *Publishers Weekly* bestselling author from Indiana. She gave up a career in the corporate world to write about sexy billionaires and alpha bad boys. With over twenty books, three series, and many awards beneath her belt, she's never regretted her choice to live out her dream. She's a free spirit, a wanderer at heart, and loves animals with a passion. When she's not tripping over random objects, you'll find her walking in the sunshine with her rambunctious dogs and dreaming about true love. Subscribe to Jeana's newsletter and get the inside scoop on new and upcoming releases, giveaways, and much more! SUBSCRIBE

www.ingramcontent.com/pod-product-compliance
Lightning Source LLC
Chambersburg PA
CBHW071144180726
48291CB00007B/2331